MIDNIGHT AMBUSH...

The man bought Raider a drink. When he began to cough, Raider said they should step outside. By now it was dark. The only ones around were two men leaning on the rail, looking out into the darkness, the way people like to do on a ship.

The fourth man casually followed them out of the saloon, apparently unnoticed by Raider. It was all going down so naturally and smoothly, it seemed to the four men too good to be true . . .

At a nod from the man with Raider, he and one gun at the rail grabbed the Pinkerton's arms. The third man at the rail drove his fist in Raider's gut and, when he doubled over, kneed him in the face. Then all four lifted the kicking, struggling Pinkerton and tossed him over the deck rail.

All that was left on the deck was a black Stetson.

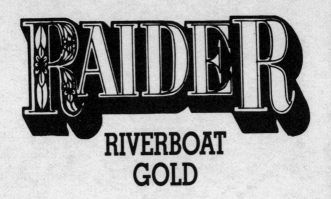

RAIDER

RIVERBOAT
GOLD

J.D. HARDIN

B

BERKLEY BOOKS, NEW YORK

RIVERBOAT GOLD

A Berkley Book/published by arrangement with
the author

PRINTING HISTORY
Berkley edition/November 1988

ISBN: 0-425-11195-4

A BERKLEY BOOK ® TM 757,375
Berkley Books are published by the Berkley Publishing Group,
200 Madison Avenue, New York, NY 10016
The name "BERKLEY" and the "B" logo
are trademaks belonging to the Berkley Publishing Corporation.

PRINTED IN THE UNITED STATES OF AMERICA

10 9 8 7 6 5 4 3 2 1

CHAPTER ONE

The two Pinkerton operatives looked out the windows of the train at the flat fields of Wisconsin. They were on their way from Chicago to St. Paul, Minnesota. In the fields, dairy cows chewing their cud gazed at the train.

"Take your last look at peace and quiet," one of the Pinkertons told the other. "Work with Raider will be like being in a room with a mad dog."

"I been lookin' forward to it," the second operative said. "I expect to learn a lot from him."

"From that loco son of a bitch? All you'll learn from him is how to get yourself booted out of the agency. I have it on good sources that the only reason Mr. Pinkerton tolerates him is for dirty work."

"He's the agency's top gun."

"That's what I said—dirty work."

"You been listenin' to stories put out by people jealous of Raider," said the second operative, whose name was Tom Magnuson. "Sure, Mr. Pinkerton wouldn't tolerate you or me if we did what Raider does. Mr. Pinkerton wouldn't tolerate shit from the people who told you these things, which is what makes them jealous of Raider. That varmint does what he pleases, and Mr. Pinkerton can like it or lump it—the one thing he can't do is fire the best man in the agency."

"He's done it," his partner, whose name was Warren Trent, pointed out.

"Only to hire him back an hour later. Most times, it was Raider who quit and Mr. Pinkerton had to practically get on his knees and beg him to come back." Tom grinned. "When I get real good, maybe I'll try givin' Mr. Pinkerton a hard time too."

"He'll kick your butt, no matter how good you get."

"I know," Tom agreed sadly.

In spite of what Warren Trent said, he was looking forward to working with the legendary Pinkerton operative just as much as Tom was, only Warren didn't intend to show it, not to Tom and not to Raider. On this job they were all going to be equals, so far as Warren was concerned. He'd maybe boast later about having been a partner of the famous gun-toting Pinkerton, but he wasn't going to give any hero worship to the man while he was around. The way Tom was behaving, Raider was going to walk all over him.

Tom said, "I reckon Raider's just going to take one look at us two and bust out laughin'—if he don't get mad."

This annoyed Warren. He knew as well as Tom that Raider had the reputation of sneaking off and leaving inexperienced agents standing. He had put one operative on an eastbound train with the impression it was headed west: the operative was still waiting for the Rockies to appear when the train neared Chicago. Well, Raider was not going to treat Warren Trent that way. Tom could kiss ass if he wanted to. Warren intended to prove himself.

The train got into St. Paul at 2:35 in the afternoon. Both Pinkertons carried only one piece of hand baggage, and they were soon free of the throng sorting out their belongings on the platform. Two men approached them, hard-faced men with cold eyes.

"Pardon me," the one in a black derby said. "Any chance you two gentlemen are the Pinkertons for Mallory Trust?"

"What of it if we are?" Warren wanted to know.

"We're the Mallory guards, sir. We been sent to show you the way. Can I take your bag, sir?"

"No. I can manage it," Warren said brusquely.

All the same, he was pleased by the looks of these two. The one with the derby had a broken nose and one missing eyebrow. The other man was huge, red-faced, and hamfisted. If there was going to be trouble, these were the kind of men Warren wanted to have on his side. Warren would never have openly admitted it, but he knew Tom was right in suggesting that their own appearances were not too impressive —or at least not terribly frightening. Even when Warren felt mean inside, people just saw his cheerful harmless-looking exterior. People never even knew when he was in a bad mood! Tom's appearance was even less threatening than his own. This would be no problem for most people, but it was a real headache to be a Pinkerton and look soft. If a man looked mean, people didn't try things with him—although he might in reality be a poor fighter. But when, in spite of himself, a man looked friendly and open, people stepped right in. Nobody would mess with these two bank guards.

The men led them along a couple of streets, down a side street, along another busy street, then down a narrow alley. Warren was right behind them, and he felt steel before he saw it when the man in the derby whirled around on him. The sharp pain in his chest struck first, then he looked down to see the blade in the man's hand as it was being pushed into his insides. Warren knew he was watching himself being murdered, and he certainly felt the agony of it in his chest, but his arms wouldn't work to draw his gun or strike back with his fists, and his legs wouldn't work so he could back away.

Tom Magnuson couldn't believe he was seeing his partner being butchered like this before his eyes. He was hauling out his Smith & Wesson pistol when the other man set upon him. The big, red-faced man had been lethargic up to this point. Now he moved fast as a snake. He slashed Tom across the knuckles with his knife, but this did not make the Pinkerton drop his gun.

Tom snapped back the hammer and took the blade point in his upper arm before he could squeeze the trigger. The blade must have severed a tendon, because his fingers retracted into a claw and the gun fell from his hand to the cobbles. The big man plunged the knife three times in Tom's chest. He fell facedown, clutching at himself, feeling his warm blood running through his fingers. The pain was awful. Then it began to slacken, and Tom knew that he was dying.

"Go through his pockets," the man in the derby ordered. "Take everything. I'll search this one."

"I say we go right now and pick up the gold," the big man said.

"An' I say we do things the way we was ordered to," the man in the derby said. "There's supposed to be a third Pinkerton comin' in. If we show up early with just two of us, it may get someone suspicious. Let's do it the way we're supposed to. Meet this dumbbell at the railroad station. The bank's open till nine tonight. His train is due in at five. Where's it comin' from?"

The big man consulted some of the papers he had taken from Tom Magnuson's pockets. "Omaha. We meet him directly under the clock in the station."

Raider left the train from Omaha and entered the station, scanning it for the clock where he was supposed to meet the two Pinkerton agents who he had been sent to help with the gold shipment. Why, after all this time had he agreed to work as a team again? he asked himself.

Just getting soft, I guess—soft in the head.

William Wagner, Allan Pinkerton's right-hand man, had been the one to talk him into it. Wagner and his damned bottle of prime bourbon.

"Just a little celebration over the success of that last operation," Wagner had coaxed. Raider was not one to refuse a drink, and Wagner had appeared to be in an unusually jovial mood. There was another bottle in Wagner's desk to follow the first.

Raider poured himself a drink and pushed the bottle toward Wagner.

"No, thanks. Drink up, Raider. You deserve it. Me, my health's not what it used to be. I think I'll go easy for a little while."

With a grunt of satisfaction Raider tossed back the shot. The liquor was beginning to warm his innards. He stretched out his long legs and relaxed in his chair.

That's when the son of a bitch had begun working on him. Pleading with him, as a *personal favor* to Mr. Pinkerton. Raider, in the warm glow of plenty of praise and alcohol, had agreed to shepherd the two agents and the gold from St. Paul to New Orleans.

Damn. Now he was regretting it. They were probably greenhorns or stupid or something of the sort. Wagner hadn't told him much about them and he was prepared for the worst.

The two men were already beneath the clock when the train from Omaha pulled into the station. They scanned the people walking along the platform from the train, looking for someone like the two men they had met before. They saw two likely candidates— well—groomed young men who looked as if they had been strictly brought up, stepping lively with an easy air—but neither one came over to stand beneath the clock or even glance that way. As the stream of passengers along the platform thinned, the two men found themselves beneath the clock with just about the last kind of person they expected to be a Pinkerton operative—a big, sun-bronzed, leathery-skinned man who looked as if he had stepped out of Dodge City with a big pistol on his right hip and a long gun wrapped in a swathe of buckskin under his left arm. His black hat, black leather jacket, sun-bleached denims, and western boots marked him as man who did not spend much time in cities. His piercing black eyes, above his luxuriant black mustaches, marked him as a man dangerous to cross.

The man in the derby said hopefully to him, "Ain't no chance you're a Pinkerton, is there?"

"Matter of fact, I am. Name's Raider." He smiled in a resigned but friendly way which made him look less fierce. "You gents have identification papers." They showed them to him. "Tom Magnuson, pleased to meet you." He shook hands with the man in the derby, then peered at the other man's papers and shook his hand. "Warren Trent, it's a pleasure. Like I said, the name's Raider." He fumbled around in his pockets and produced a battered piece of paper, folded many times. Having carefully opened it out, he spread it on one knee. "It's been a bit hard t' read since I fell in a river and had t' dry it out in the sun. But you see my name there, almost faded out."

"Your identification is fine with Tom and me, Raider," Warren said. "What do you say we go and get the job done?"

"Fine by me," Raider said agreeably. "You boys come as a surprise to me. I thought you must be waitin' for someone else under the clock. It sure is a change to have grown men assigned to me as partners. Mostly it's kids they send. They ain't hardly any full grown adults in the detective agency anymore. Mr. Pinkerton must be takin' 'em out o' the schoolrooms. I guess the grown ones get sense an' quit, while they're still in one piece, except for the ones like us, who I expect will never get sense. Where you boys been workin'?"

"Oh, eh, on the railroads," Warren said. "Both of us," he added, saving Tom the need to think up an answer.

"I been after horse thieves," Raider said. "I brought two of 'em in t' the town o' Hillsdale, just this side o' Cheyenne. It took me four days o' ridin' day an' night to run them critters in at gunpoint, an' it took less than an hour after we reached town for the citizens of Hillsdale to string 'em up without a trial. They almost strung me up too, when I tried to stop 'em."

The two men said nothing, only looked unhappily at each other. They regarded themselves as rough and tough, but like everyone in midwestern and eastern cities, they considered themselves several notches above the highest form of life to be found out west. This casual talk about lynching horse thieves unnerved them. And this character looked to them like *he* might have murdered some Pinkerton and was now passing himself off with his papers.

"That would be a good one all right," the man with the derby said to the other in a quiet voice as they walked behind Raider on a crowded sidewalk. "If we was both pullin' the same trick on each other. How would it end up?"

"Maybe better than it will if he's for real," Warren said. "I don't like the looks of him. But we stick with the plan. That will see us through."

The gold bullion was packed in wood crates. The ten-pound bars were packed in straw, ten to a crate. There were three crates, which made a total of three hundred pounds of 24-carat gold, 98 or 99 percent pure. Raider insisted on opening every crate and checking every bar.

"I don't want to be guardin' any bars o' lead slipped in here by some o' you slick bankers," Raider told the manager of First Mallory Trust. "Before we sign for this stuff and take it out o' your vault, we're goin' to be sure we ain't been had by city shysters."

The manager's mouth tightened. He had already tried to intimidate Raider, with a notable lack of success. Now he kept quiet.

Raider nailed the crates shut, tossed one on his left shoulder and walked out of the vault, through the back, to the street door, and set the crate down on the wagon they had hired. The other two carried a crate between them and heaved it onto the wagon. They were followed by two bank guards with the last crate. After the three Pinkertons signed the bank's papers acknowledging receipt of the gold, Raider gave orders to the driver to head for the *Burlington Queen*, which was waiting for them at the docks. Two mangy horses, with their ribs showing, pulled

the wagon with four men and three wood crates—
not an impressive sight and certainly not one suggesting to people on the street that a fortune in gold
was passing them by.

Raider's orders were to deliver, with the help of
his two partners, the bullion to a shipping company
in New Orleans; from there it would be sent to
France. The *Burlington Queen* would take them
down the Mississippi as far as St. Louis. There they
would change to another steamer bound for New Orleans. Raider had no great love for water—either in
a drinking glass or as a replacement for solid ground
—but this assignment looked to him like a pleasant
change of pace from hours in the saddle and days on
board trains, and at the end of it was New Orleans, a
town which had never disappointed him yet.

The river was not wide, and on the other bank lay
Minneapolis. Traffic between the Twin Cities was
heavy, with passengers and merchandise being ferried across the water in both directions in crafts of all
sizes and shapes. The *Burlington Queen* was tied up
alongside a busy dock. Its big paddlewheels were located at midpoint on the sides, and the four decks
were ornamented with fluted columns and white rail-
ing work, like a Southern planter's mansion. The pilothouse jutted out in front as a wide-windowed
balcony. Of necessity, this sidewheeler was much
smaller than the huge sternwheelers that plied the
river's lower reaches, because the Mississippi up
here was shallow and winding, with dangerous rapids
and shifting sand bars.

When the wagon pulled up to the gangplank,
Raider jumped down saying, "Our passages have
been reserved, but I want a look at where they intend
to stow these boxes."

He cursed as his right boot landed in horse dung.
He scraped his sole clean on the wood spokes of a

rear wagon wheel and walked up the gangplank to the deck. He was taken below decks to the hold and shown the so-called strong room, which a determined child could have broken into. Raider decided that the crates would be safer in full view, stacked one upon the other. That way they could be checked frequently with no more than a glance, and anyone interfering with them would not be provided with cover. When Raider came up on deck again, the wagon was gone.

He ran down the gangplank and found the wagon driver lying on the ground, surrounded by a small group of people. He was bleeding from a cut over his right eye and was still stunned. Raider didn't wait to exchange words with anyone. He rushed across the street to where a fine bay gelding was standing harnessed to an empty buggy. Raider freed him from between the shafts of the buggy, unhitched him and sprang on his back. Unused to riders, the horse bucked and reared. Raider pulled hard on the reins, holding him hard, digging his spurless heels into the horse's sides, letting him know who was master. When the animal bolted, Raider loosened the reins and let him run.

Raider battered his balls bouncing on the lean bare back of the cantering horse, which didn't sweeten his mood any. The wagon had turned away from the docks, probably at the first street. Raider tried to turn the horse into it, but didn't succeed. He went on twisting and yanking the horse's head to the right, so that if the reins didn't give, either the horse's neck or Raider's hand had to. Forcing the horse to take the second turnoff, Raider almost fell when the son of a bitch scraped his left leg against a building. Raider wondered if this was a trick the horse knew well. He had seen several men crushed against corral rails by mean horses with good brains.

The cobbled streets were lined with warehouses

and choked with loaded and empty wagons squeezing by each other. Raider could make better headway with the horse by weaving in and out among the slow-moving wagons. The horse quieted some— having no other choice, since he could hardly leap over wagons. Raider soothed the gelding by talking to him and patting his neck.

The Pinkerton passed a newsboy on a corner, hawking the evening papers. He remembered now what he had heard newsboys calling earlier, and had paid little attention to at the time. Two unidentified young men had been found murdered in an alley near the railroad station. Raider suddenly had a gut feeling that their names would turn out to be Warren Trent and Tom Magnuson, of the Pinkerton National Detective Agency. Raider considered himself a fool to have accepted those two hard-boiled imposters as Pinkerton operatives. It was this goddamn city. It was making him lose his mind. Raider cursed the Twin Cities and all the city slickers in them.

He heard shouts and curses from one street where the wagon traffic was backed up and not moving. That was what he was looking for. Down the street a distance, a wagon had lost a wheel and was blocking traffic. There was no room for Raider's horse to weave in and out between the stationary wagons, so Raider pulled him onto the sidewalk, whooped, and slapped his rump with the reins. It did Raider's soul a world of good to gallop plainsman-style along the sidewalk, yelling, driving the townies into doorways or beneath wagons to get out from under his horse's hooves.

He saw the big man who had called himself Tom Magnuson stand up on the disabled wagon and draw the Smith & Wesson pistol he had taken from the dead Pinkerton.

At the sight of the gun in the big man's hand,

Raider hauled out his long-barreled Remington .44
and snapped off two shots across his horse's neck.
The horse didn't appreciate the two explosions inches
away from his ears—in fact, the gelding went crazy.
In a full jump, with all four hooves off the ground,
he flexed his back in a sudden twist that threw his
rider.

The heavy Pinkerton crashed down on his back
ten feet away on a wagonload of sacks. His impact
ruptured the sacks he landed on, and golden streams
of oats leaked out all over the wagon. The driver was
too astounded to curse. Raider had noticed that about
city people before. The least little thing which was
unexpected left them at a complete loss.

He jumped up and ran to the disabled wagon. The
other man, who had called himself Warren Trent, had
broken open the top of one crate with his pistol butt
and was reaching inside with his left hand. This man
had been given a chance to escape after his partner
was shot and Raider was thrown. But he had seen
those gold bars in the vault, and he wasn't willing to
leave unless he was carrying one. Raider put a bullet
in his ribs.

The impostor screamed and dropped the pistol to
clutch his wound, but he went on rooting in the crate
with his left hand, trying to drag a ten-pound gold
bar out. The man's greed was so overpowering that it
had blinded him to the fact that the lead in his gut
was more important to him than the gold in his hand.

Raider didn't want that gold bar displayed in pub-
lic. He doubted he would be able to prevent a mob
from looting the crates if it became known what was
in them. He leaned the heel of his gun hand on the
back of his left hand, looked quickly down his revolver's sights and squeezed the trigger.

The .44 bullet struck the man's wrist, almost tearing the hand free of the arm. With his left hand dan-

gling from skin and ligaments, the man screamed again and rolled off the wagon.

Raider waved his smoking weapon at some frightened onlookers. "Get that wheel back on that wagon. You! And You! Lift that wagon up. Mister, get down here quick and fit that wheel if you got plans to see daylight tomorrow."

"It ain't no good fella," one man whined fearfully. "The peg in the axle holdin' the wheel on is missin'."

"No, it ain't," Raider said. He reached in a pocket and produced the peg. He said to the uncomprehending man, "It was just a simple precaution I took before I stepped on that boat. Guess I ain't no sailor. Water makes me wary."

CHAPTER TWO

Raider spent all night settling with the law. That was another bother a man had in cities—he couldn't just talk with the marshal or sheriff and settle things in a straightforward way, there was a whole police department involved and about twenty different fellows with brass buttons and red noses had to be separately told the whole story and deliver their weighty opinion on what should be done. By the time Raider was done with some of them, they were all for jailing him. It was the sight of three hundred pounds of pure gold that finally overcame them all. They could understand that easily enough. Gold explained things better to them than words. They released him just in time to catch the *Burlington Queen*. One benefit of this night-long ordeal was that the newspapers had not yet been given the full story at the time he boarded the boat, so no one on board knew what was in those three crates or that he was a Pinkerton. At least, he hoped not.

The sun rose as the boat headed downriver from St. Paul. Raider leaned on the deck rail and saw the last of the city buildings along the river banks: old

St. Paul on the east and the new city of Minneapolis on the west. Soon there was nothing to be seen on either bank, except a wilderness of forest, with rocks and sand next to the water, which was dark green and fast-moving. Fort Snelling came up on the west bank, and below it the Minnesota River joined the Mississippi, the mingling currents twisting into sinister whirlpools. Sometimes the main channel ran close to the bank, and basking turtles on exposed tree roots popped into the water as the boat moved near them.

Raider passed the time talking with a German who had spent ten years in Pennsylvania before moving to Minnesota the previous year. He told Raider that the pay was better in Minnesota and that the land, livestock, and food were all cheaper than back east. He was working for a farmer downriver at Red Wing, but in a year or two he expected to have a place of his own; then he could think about getting married and raising a family—he would need some sons to help with the work.

People who lived their lives according to plan intrigued Raider. Living from hour to hour and day to day as he did, he regarded them as an alien race. Raider easily understood cowboys, gamblers, miners, even whores—insofar as any man could understand a woman. What Raider couldn't understand was why some folks preferred the settled life. Raider's family had been sodbusters in Arkansas. From his recollections, a farmer's life hadn't been much more secure than a gambler's, and the work was a helluva lot harder.

The river narrowed as it ran between bluffs, forested down to the water's edge, interrupted by outcrops of gray rock. The boat followed the channel among long narrow islands; often it seemed to be headed straight for the swamp oak and tamarack on the bank, only at the last moment giving way to a hidden channel opening. Likewise, occasional boats heading upstream would emerge from the forest. Below the bluffs, the river widened into a slough two miles across, with islands scattered everywhere; then more bluffs and an Indian encampment on one shore, with the smoke from the cooking fires rising straight up in the air. The river made a dogleg eastward, then a sharp turn south. The warehouses of Red Wing were on the west bank. The wheat farmers farther west brought their grain here by wagon and shipped it downstream. The German told Raider that in ten years Red Wing would be bigger than St. Paul.

He said goodbye to the German and wished him luck. Raider kept an eye on the new passengers who boarded. There weren't many, and only one was of interest to the Pinkerton. He was a big, lean riverman who nodded in a surly way to the crewmen on the *Burlington Queen*. They nodded back to him cautiously. It was clear that they knew each other, and that this lone man put the fear of God in the crew. He roamed the ship, apparently searching for somebody. When his eyes rested on Raider—though it was only for a split second—the Pinkerton knew the man had been looking for him.

It had been too much to hope that he would have been let alone with a shipment of three hundred pounds of gold. Whoever knew about the gold and had the two Pinkertons intercepted from the Chicago train also intended to take the gold from him on the river. Raider had telegraphed a report to Chicago from St. Paul and had received a reply just before leaving. Two more men would be at St. Louis to help him transfer the gold to a larger steamer, and would ride with him downriver. Raider hadn't been pleased to learn that the murdered Pinkerton agents would be replaced.

He preferred working solo. He didn't have to

waste most of his effort in saving the skins of partners who were supposed to be there to help him. This way there was only one hide to save, and that was his own. But back in St. Paul he had too much on his mind to argue about it.

That night he lay his bedroll on the floor of the hold, next to the crates. Then he went to the saloon to drink, coming down to the hold every so often to make sure the gold was all right. He soon wearied of doing this and hired a boy for a nickel an hour to sit in the hold and keep watch. He told the boy he was a scout from the Army, that there were Indian treaties drawn up on buffalo hide in the crates, that the Army and the government would jail him for years if he let anything happen to them. The boy blinked with fright; however, the lure of a nickel an hour for doing nothing was too tempting for the boy to refuse.

Blindside got his name from killing a one-eyed gambler on a riverboat while he was still a kid—the gambler never saw the knife coming for his ribs on his blind side until it was too late. He was well known in all the river towns from St. Paul down to Muscatine and beyond. A crooked lawyer he often worked with in Red Wing advanced him a hundred dollars to collect three crates off the *Burlington Queen*. Only one man was guarding them, a big cowpuncher with black mustaches and a sixgun. He'd need to be taken care of. When Blindside unloaded the crates in the nearest river town possible, he would be paid another four hundred dollars. Someone would be watching him.

Normally Blindside would have decided this was a bullshit deal with something hidden in it. He'd have taken the hundred in advance and skipped. But the Red Wing lawyer who had hired him was not a man to treat lightly. He paid well, his jobs were genuine, he knew people who could take care of Blindside if he tried any tricks. So he boarded the *Burlington Queen* at Red Wing, looked over the passengers, and easily spotted the big cowpuncher with the sixgun.

He saw the crates in the hold, the cowpuncher's bedding spread next to them, and the kid the cowpuncher hired to watch them, while Raider was drinking in the saloon. This was going to be easy. He could make five hundred overnight. Blindside knew men who worked a year to make that.

There was a swell running on Lake Pepin, which was the widest and longest pool on the entire Mississippi. The boat pointed into the waves, lurching from stem to stern, chasing half the drinkers out of the saloon to empty their guts over the side. The crew walked unconcernedly among the ill passengers and ignored their desperate pleas to be put ashore, telling them, "This ain't nothin'. You should see what it's like when we have a real blow."

Blindside wasn't much bothered by it, and he noticed that the cowpuncher showed no signs of leaving the saloon. Tired of having the bottle slide away from him along the bar, Raider had quit using a glass and was now holding the neck of the bottle and drinking from it. The son of a bitch was big and he could hold his whiskey, but Blindside knew he could take him. Maybe not on dry land. But no one could stand against a riverman on board a boat. This man looked like a fighter but he was no riverman.

Finally the whiskey and the lurching of the boat against the waves seemed to affect the cowpuncher. He stuffed the bottle in a pocket of his leather jacket and made his way across the pitching deck to the rail. It was dark, with light rain spitting in the cluster of lamps at the bow which the captain used for navigation. The big man was almost halfway down the ship, in front of one of the side paddles, leaning on the rail and looking down into the dark water. Only one person was near him, a man violently retching over the side. He would be too busy with his own concerns to pay much attention.

Blindside saw that now was the right moment. He had done it a number of times before. It was only a matter of a few seconds work, so fast indeed that if done correctly, no one could be quite sure what happened. They might even think he had been trying to rescue the man.

The riverman hurried back into the saloon and made his way to a door just behind where the big cowpuncher was leaning on the rail. He came out the door fast, crept silently up behind the cowpuncher, and hooked him by the right ankle. The riverman used all his strength to lift him by the right leg and then shoulder him over the waist-high rail.

But as the cowpuncher was going over the rail, he clung to it and kicked backward with both feet, like a mule. The heels of Raider's boots caught Blindside in the belly. He staggered backward across the deck. Using the next wave's roll, he waited for the deck to pitch up, then came charging back when the deck sank down again, intending to use his momentum and weight on the downward slope to heave the cowpuncher over the side. The big man was still leaning on the rail with his side to him. He moved amazingly fast for a man his size, stepping backward an instant before Blindside's shoulder would have struck him. The riverman found only empty air where the man's bulky body would have been. If the rail had been a foot higher, it would have stopped him. It didn't. He had no time to cry out as the deck sank to its lowest point and he was pitched through the air, down into the river water, which closed over his head.

Raider looked over the rail and saw the riverman's

head and shoulder emerge in the foamy wash alongside the boat. The man in the water looked upward a
moment, then behind him, just in time to see the
revolving paddle blades bearing down on him. The
wood blades chopped him beneath the surface.

The Pinkerton waited to see if the body would be
lifted on the paddlewheel. When it wasn't, he knew
there was nothing much he could do. No one seemed
to have noticed anything. The man at the rail twenty
paces away was still vomiting over the side. Raider
took a swallow from his whiskey bottle and replaced
it in his pocket. Who the hell had hired the riverman?
And the two killers in St. Paul? Where was he getting his information from? Was he aboard the *Burlington Queen?*

Raider sensed that he was being watched at that
very moment. Something made him look up to the
deck above the one he was on. A man with a dour
expression and a riverman's peaked cap was staring
down at him. Raider stared back up at him, and the
man turned away. He walked forward along the deck
rail and entered the pilothouse. Raider realized that
this man had witnessed everything—and he wasn't
going to do anything about it. Not for the moment, at
least.

Not one to brood overlong on unanswerable questions, Raider headed back into the saloon, put his
bottle on the bar, and asked for a glass. He had just
poured himself a drink and set the bottle back on the
bar when a beautiful woman in a bright yellow silk
dress rose from a table and came to stand beside him.
She nodded to the barkeep, and he slid an empty
glass along the countertop to her. She half filled her
glass with whiskey from Raider's bottle, replaced it,
and returned to her table without a glance or a word
in Raider's direction.

She had acted so suddenly that Raider couldn't

think of anything appropriate to say to her. Had Doc Weatherbee, his old partner, been in his place, he would have said something clever and would soon have had her laughing and relaxed, thinking he was the greatest fellow in the world. Raider was a man of few words. He just didn't know what to say to women a lot of the time.

In a short while the woman in the yellow dress was back at the bar again. This time she held onto her glass, waiting for him to pour her a drink. Raider obliged, running his eyes over her pretty face, her curly black hair, her long sensuous fingers, and delicate hands, and the uppermost parts of her full breasts. She hardly looked at him, said nothing, and went back to the table with her drink. Once more, Raider hadn't been able to think of a damn thing to say. If she came back again, he'd ask her name.

He didn't have to. Not long after she sat down at her table, she and the other woman who was sitting with her began to squabble. This woman called her a whore several times. She rose, and this time approached Raider without a glass in her hand.

"You hear that bitch?" she asked him. "She called me a whore."

"So?" Raider asked, puzzled. He had assumed they were both whores and saw nothing to argue about.

"Did I ask you for money?" she shouted.

"You ain't said a word to me till just now," he answered.

"See?" she shouted to the woman at the table.

"Whore!" the other woman yelled back.

"I'm gonna kill the bitch," she told Raider and headed back to the table.

The other woman rose to meet her. They grappled for a few moments, until the woman in the yellow dress grabbed the other woman's hair, pulled her to her knees and cracked her head against the side of the wooden table top, leaving her sitting on the floor, her mouth hanging open in a dazed way. The woman in the yellow dress picked up her glass and headed back to Raider at the bar.

The men in the saloon gave her a round of applause. There was nothing more entertaining than seeing a good fight. They were surprised it was over so quickly, being used to fights between women dragging on, with the words harder than the blows. They applauded a job nicely done, and several went over to help the vanquished woman back to her seat.

"I'm Marie," the woman said to Raider. "Did the bitch scratch me or tear anything?" she asked, turning around for his inspection.

Raider examined her closely. "You look prime quality to me."

"Mister, I ain't a goddamn steer, in case you haven't noticed. Beef is prime quality, I guess. Now what would you call me?"

"A high stepper?"

"I ain't a horse neither, but it's better than being a cow. What's your name?" When he told her, she asked, "What you got in them crates? Gold?"

"Sure," Raider said, without missing a beat. "My life savings."

"You ain't gonna tell me? I'm a curious person, Raider. You got me kind of intrigued. You ain't sneaky enough to be a gambler, and you ain't crazy enough to be a gunfighter. Know what I figure you to be? A lawman."

Raider laughed. "You're kidding."

"No, I ain't. A girl like me needs to be a fast judge of men. I am. Ain't but two men ever fooled me. Both of 'em were gamblers, and now I stay away from any man too handy with a deck of cards. Maybe I was right when I guessed there's gold in them crates—else why would you have the kid guarding 'em while you're here?"

"Who told you that?" Raider asked, with a serious edge to his voice.

"I saw for myself. I don't miss a thing."

"So I'm a lawman with three crates of gold. Where does that leave us?"

"I'm a business girl headed for St. Louis. Been a year since I did anything for fun. You won't have to open them crates to pay me."

He followed her to her private cabin. She had him undo the hooks at the back of her dress, slipped out of it, and stood naked before him. Raider ran his hands over her smooth skin, stroked her breasts, then her buttocks. He wondered if she was luring him here while her confederates pillaged the crates. Or was she just joking about the gold, thinking he was playing along? Well, even if they did steal the gold from the crates, they would still be on board with it. One thing he could be sure of—nobody was going to swim off with all that gold. So he let his mind get back to more immediate things. . . .

Marie had long legs and a soft black curly bush. She clung tightly to him as his skilled fingers manipulated and stroked her, sending tingling sensations through her flesh and wildly exciting her. When she was no longer able to resist his tantalizing touch, she pulled him on top of her on the narrow bunk, and pushed his stiff member into her cunt, moaning loudly as he penetrated her. At each thrust of his staff, she panted and moaned. For Raider it was go with the flow, gliding downriver. . . .

CHAPTER THREE

A wind suddenly blew up while the steamer was on Lake Pepin. In this wide section of the river, the water rose into five-foot waves which crashed against the boat, violent as any storm at sea. The cabin lurched and pitched, and Raider was thrown ass-naked out of Marie's bunk onto his head on the floor. For a confused moment he thought she had flung him out somehow. Then the floor pitched sharply once more and he rapped his head on the wall.

"Dang it, Marie, if we're goin' to sink an' drown, like I think we are, I want to see what's happenin' to me. I don't want my lungs to fill with water while I'm locked in this box. The way these walls move up and down gives me the willies. And when they find my body, I want them to find it with my clothes on, and my boots and my gun." He had a hard time keeping his balance while pulling his pants on. "Won't you come to the saloon deck with me?"

"Naw, I always figured on dying in bed—with no clothes on," she added. "I hope I ain't been in the water too long when they find my body. I want them fellers to enjoy looking at me."

"I reckon they will," he said and went out the cabin door.

He looked out into the stormy night from inside the saloon. Moonlight shone on ragged rows of surf-topped waves. Water and spray lashed across the decks, preventing Raider from going out for fear of being swept overboard. He saw a crewman staring out a porthole, smoking a pipe.

"Mighty bad out there," the Pinkerton observed, wondering what the crewman's opinion was, but not wanting to look a coward in fear of drowning.

"You often get a blow on Pepin," the crewman said, calmly puffing his pipe. "This is nothing much. She's just giving her ass a scratch."

The waves grew bigger, and the steamer nosed into them, bucking like a bronc. Raider was fairly sure he was going to meet his maker, but he had thought this often enough before without ever getting killed. Other passengers stayed wedged in corners where they would not get thrown around. Down in the hold, Raider found the boy he had hired sitting up, wide-eyed and frightened, on the bedding next to the crates. He gave him a reassuring smile and went back to watch the waves again, waiting for the one with a trick twist which would cause the paddle-wheeler to founder.

Just before dawn, the boat reached the place where the lake narrowed into the river once more, and the steamer came out of the breakers, into calm water. For a while, Raider had to get used to not feeling the deck pitching beneath his feet. Then the sun came up on the eastern bank. Ten minutes later, the wind had died totally. It was the beginning of a hot, still day.

At Wabasha the steamer nosed in to the town wharf. Neat blocks of redbrick stores and houses were under construction a distance from the river.

Closer to the river there was nothing but huts made from driftwood and mud. If floodwaters took these there would be no great loss. Probably no one would miss the occupants either.

Raider watched those leaving and boarding the steamer. He reckoned that maybe half the oncoming passengers were cutthroats of one kind or another. He noticed a small, pudgy man who had earlier left the steamer hurry back down the wharf and get on board, tipping the crewman at the gangplank for waiting for him. Raider idly wondered what he had hurried ashore for—there were more loose women, card games, and liquor aboard the *Burlington Queen* than in all of the town of Wabasha.

There was something different about the kid he had paid to guard his crates. Raider wasn't quite sure at first, then he spotted it.

"You're his brother, ain't you?" he asked. "You're not the one who hired on with me."

"There's three of us, sir. We all been working for you."

It wasn't until he saw all three of them together that Raider believed this. There was less than a year between each two of them in age. Except for a noticeable difference in size between the oldest and the youngest when they were together, they might have been triplets. They were traveling down to St. Louis, where their uncle had a hardware store doing good business and in need of willing workers. Raider left it to them to decide among themselves how to share out their round-the-clock guard on the crates, and he gave them Marie's cabin number in case they needed him urgently and couldn't find him in the saloon or on deck.

With that taken care of, Raider decided on a hand of poker. He passed most of the day at the game, except when he took time off to stroll the decks with Marie. She didn't gamble, so she spent most of her time sipping drinks and talking with the other women, including the one who had called her a whore the previous day.

The steamer called into Fountain City, Winona, and Trempealeau, hitting some fast rapids on the way. The boat traveled headlong down them, sometimes passing others barely moving in the opposite direction. Islands of all sizes, often with tall trees growing on them, were scattered all over, as were bare sandbars. The main channel wound in and out among them.

A man who boarded the steamer at La Crosse, Wisconsin, joined the card game, lost money, and accused Raider of cheating.

"Then I ain't much of a cheat," the Pinkerton said, "because I didn't win that damn pot, nor the one before it."

"The cards are marked," the man claimed. He was a big raw-looking man who looked odd in his expensive city clothes.

"If they're marked," Raider suggested, "you better ask who supplied them. I didn't."

"I been watching you," the man said accusingly.

"Watch me all you want. But I ain't sittin' at this table to hold a conversation with you, mister. Play cards or stand up and let someone who wants to play take your chair."

The Pinkerton was fast losing his good humor. When the man left the table, it was not a moment too soon.

After he had gone, one of the other players said, "If he had called *me* a cheat, I'd have made him answer for it."

Raider smiled. "Maybe I'd 've took it to heart if I was really cheatin', but hell, I ain't even winnin'.

I'm not the one who took his money from him. I figure him as kind of crazy, and I can't see the point of fightin' a man on account o' that."

"No man calls me a cheat and walks away with a smile on his face," the other card player insisted.

"Well, I guess you're a sight meaner than I am," Raider told him.

This made the players laugh, because Raider was twice as big and rough as the man who was talking. They all agreed that the man who had called him a cheat must be crazy. They went on with the poker game and did not stop when a fiddle and accordian started up and dancing began. Raider left the game for a while to dance with Marie, but he wasn't much of a dancer and he got back to the card table without too much delay. As soon as he was seated, the raw-looking man in the city clothes, the one who had called him a cheat, asked Marie for the next dance.

They danced for a long while, but this didn't bother Raider. He kept to his card game, and never looked their way, even when they were dancing close by.

The man was getting impatient.

"Bob," Marie said to him, "seems to me we're spending a lot of time over near this card game. You dancing with me or trying to make one of those players jealous?"

"If he cared about you, he'd have done something by now. He mustn't think you're worth much if he lets another man dance with you all this time."

"If that's all you do, I reckon he don't care," Marie said.

"You want to go to a cabin with me?" he asked.

"No."

"I'll pay real good."

"I ain't whoring this trip, Bob, I'm on vacation. Now you make up your mind. Either you put your mind on our dancing or you can go back to your card playing."

Bob took a while to make up his mind. Finally, he stopped dancing, saw Marie back to her table, and rejoined the card game. He was quiet until Raider won a pot. Then he exploded.

Jumping to his feet, knocking back his chair, he yelled, "Cheat! You crooked cardsharp! You do it right to my face after I warned you!"

The other players, who had been watching Raider closely since the man's previous accusation, just in case there was truth in what he said, wanted none of this. There was no way Raider could have set up the cards to win that pot—he hadn't dealt and he hadn't closely examined the other players' cards for marks while they lay on the table. In their opinion now, something else was going on. First, this fellow Bob had picked a quarrel at the table, then tried to take Raider's woman and, when that didn't work, was now making trouble at the game again. They wanted no part of it.

Raider rose slowly to his feet, never for one moment neglecting to watch the man's eyes. He wasn't staring Bob down, challenging him to do what he dared. Raider was just watching the eyes like animal things, waiting to see the telltale flicker which would indicate what their owner intended to do. Raider did not think he was carrying a gun, and he would not have much of a chance against the big Pinkerton with his bare knuckles. Listening to hardly a word the man was shouting at him, Raider watched those eyes and waited for them to tell him what would happen.

Bob's eyes flickered downward as the fingers of his right hand reached inside a vest pocket.

Raider dove for his gun, knowing at the time he was too late—he could never pull out the big Remington fast enough to outdraw a man at close quarters with a sneaky vestpocket miniature pistol.

Bob's eyes widened in surprise. His hand patted his empty vest pocket.

"You looking for this, troublemaker?" Marie called across the saloon.

Bob looked over at her and saw her holding up a little pearl-handled single-shot derringer.

"Damn pickpocket bitch took it off me during the waltz," Bob muttered. He looked at Raider and saw him unbuckling his gunbelt.

The big Pinkerton lay his gunbelt on the card table, then took off his black hat and tossed it on top of the gun. He turned to Bob and came at him in no particular hurry, his big fists clenched, his eyes blazing, and his mouth set in a hard line.

Bob got in a punch while he could, a haymaker that grazed off Raider's jaw as he pulled his head back out of its way. Bob recovered his balance quickly and connected with a straight left to Raider's gut. Expecting Raider to double over, he was bringing his right knee up to flatten his nose. But Raider's gut was muscled like a bear's and Bob's blow didn't have its intended effect. All it did was get him madder than he was before.

The Pinkerton slammed his right fist into his opponent's face and felt the man's cheekbone crack against his knuckles. He threw his weight behind another right, this time skinning his knuckles on Bob's forehead bone.

Bob's eyes rolled back in their sockets. He stepped back out of Raider's reach and shook his head vigorously to clear it. His eyes focused and he saw Raider moving in fast to put him away. He shot out a left which caught the Pinkerton in the mouth, splitting his lower lip against his teeth.

Raider eased off, seeing there was still fight left in his adversary. He wiped the blood streaming from his mouth with the back of his hand, then slammed that hand into Bob's right eye. He scored a second punch on the fractured cheekbone, which made Bob howl. Raider closed his mouth with a vicious left uppercut to the point of his chin.

The force of the blow caused Bob's teeth to snap shut like the jaws of a trap. His upper and lower front teeth clamped down on the tip of his tongue, neatly severing it. His mouth filled with blood, while the pain momentarily paralyzed him. Raider's fist in his belly didn't help. He was no longer fighting. The Pinkerton kicked his legs out from under him and loomed over him as he lay on his back on the floor. Bob saw Raider's boot raised to crash down on his leg. He tried to say something, but only a gurgle bubbled from the blood filling his mouth. He spat it out.

"Lay off me, *hombre,*" he pleaded. "Don't break my leg and I'll offer you a deal. There wasn't nothing personal about me picking a fight with you. I was sent to find you."

Raider slowly lowered his boot to the floor. "Keep talking," he said. "Who sent you?"

"Harvey Waller," Bob said.

"Who's he?"

"You don't know who Harvey Waller is?" Bob asked in wonder.

"Reckon not."

"He's the river boss down to the Illinois line, at Dubuque. Course it wasn't Harvey Waller himself who sent me, it was a feller name of Mike who works for him, runs things for him at Trempealeau. That's where I boarded this tub."

"What were you s'posed to do?" Raider asked.

Bob sat up and spat out a fresh mouthful of blood on the floor. "Take care of you, then pick up three crates and disembark at Prairie du Chien."

"You knew my name?"

"Sure. Mike told me that."

"He did?"

"Yeah. He got a telegram from Wabasha. I had to hurry to catch this boat."

Genoa, Wisconsin, was the next stop and the barkeep got Bob's tongue to stop bleeding so he could go ashore there.

The captain stood beside the wheelman on the bridge watching the river ahead like it was some living thing which, given the chance, was liable to snap back at him. His morose look never changed as he gave instructions to the wheelman from time to time and sipped from his mug of cold black coffee. He tried to ignore Raider. The man had pushed into the wheelhouse uninvited and clearly didn't give a damn about the captain being master of his ship. Had it been anyone else, the captain would have had him thrown out, but the captain had seen the man go overboard and get chomped by the paddlewheel, and he had seen the man bleeding from the mouth a few hours ago in the saloon. He was afraid. He wouldn't let the big ruffian with the three crates see that he feared him. The captain was an old hand on the river. He had seen things in his time. Among the passengers, there was always someone prone to violence on every trip. The river trade was rough. All sorts of scum floated up and down on it.

"Where's this?" Raider asked.

"Coon Slough," the captain said shortly.

They were crossing an open stretch, and the whitecaps were making the boat rock. Tree stumps stuck out of the water. In the wake of the steamer, the stumps were bared to their roots on the black river mud for a moment before the water covered them again. The channel twisted sinuously through these treacherous shallows.

"Where do we pull in next?" Raider asked.

"Lansing, on the Iowa bank." The captain gave Raider the same kind of look he was giving the mud-banks and tree stumps.

Lansing was some miles south of where the Upper Iowa River joined the Mississippi. With approving grunts from the captain, the wheelman brought the *Burlington Queen* alongside the town dock. Like all the more prosperous river towns, Lansing had some blocks of redbrick buildings, all sparkling new, some still under construction, as well as the usual collection of riverside shanties.

Raider had a fine view from the wheelhouse of who was getting on and off the steamer. The captain and wheelman stayed where they were. A few crewmen went ashore to handle the mooring ropes and help with passengers and freight. Only six passengers boarded the ship here, none of them much out of the ordinary. Only four left the ship. Raider was relieved to recognize one of them as the woman who had called Marie a whore. He waited for one of them to hurry back to the ship. None did.

As the steamer pulled out into the river, the woman Marie had fought with walked along Lansing's Main Street. She felt the ten-dollar gold piece warm in her hand. The pudgy little man had given it to her to send a telegram for him. She saw the Western Union sign just down the street.

Below Lansing, the river ran between high, wooded bluffs. Prairie du Chien, on the Wisconsin bank, was hidden from the main channel by an island on which a fur millionaire had built a manor. The shout

"Steamboat a-comin'!" was raised in the town when the *Burlington Queen* came into view. From the deck rail outside the saloon, Raider watched those getting on and off. He had wearied of his stay in the wheel-house, where the captain's coffee was as bitter and cold as his manner. No one in particular caught his eye.

The river ran between the high walls of a ravine, and the steamboat sped down over the glistening, roiling water. The stop at Prairie du Chien had been short because the captain wanted to traverse the next part of the river in daylight. There were still a couple of hours till sundown as the steamer entered Cass-ville Slough, a very wide, shallow stretch of river dotted with islands. The captain, in the wheelhouse as always, sipped on his cold coffee and grunted in-structions to the wheelman who steered a course to follow the twisting deep-water channel.

"Craft ahead," the wheelman said out of habit, knowing the captain had already seen it.

A rowboat about sixteen feet long lay right in the middle of the navigation channel, about three-quarters of a mile ahead. The captain pulled down on the cord to release steam from the warning hooter.

"Stupid bastards," he muttered and sent an order to the engine room for half speed ahead. "Even if they get out of our way in time, we're going to have to drift by them or we'll upset them in our wake and then we'll have to go back and fish them out."

"Aye, sir."

Both men left it unsaid between them that if the visibility were less clear and if fewer passengers were on deck, they would have been less concerned about the safety of the rowboat's occupants.

Two oarsmen kept the rowboat in the middle of the channel. Two more men and a woman were in

the aft section. The captain cursed again. He couldn't
drown a woman.

"Slow ahead," he ordered the engine room.

"Slow ahead, sir," the engineer's voice confirmed
through the speaking tube.

This would give the wheelman enough power to
steer the steamboat through twists in the channel.
The captain could not bring the *Burlington Queen* to
a full stop—once dead in the water, it would be
taken by the current.

"We'll go past them as best we can," he said to
the wheelman. "But worry more about the mud
banks than you do about them."

"Aye, sir."

Raider was at the rail of the lower deck as the side-
paddler neared the rowboat. The two manning the
oars pointed the bow of their small craft downstream
and rowed energetically to bring the rowboat alongside the moving steamer. The woman in the back lay
on a pile of blankets with her eyes closed.

A man next to the woman called up, "Can you
bring her to the hospital at Dubuque? Do you pull in
there? We'll pay our fares."

Crewmen threw ropes down so they could hitch
the boat alongside, a risky business because if they
did not tie themselves fast in time, they would be hit
and swamped by the huge side paddle. Then they
lowered a sling to raise the sick woman to the deck,
and lowered a rope ladder for the four men. Raider
assisted in raising the woman gently, without scraping her against the side of the steamer or, worse still,
dropping her. The men left the rowboat secured
against the side of the steamboat and climbed aboard,
the last two carrying the woman's blankets. Meanwhile Raider carried the woman to an empty cabin,

where he left her on a bunk in care of some of the women passengers. When he got back on deck, he noticed everyone gathered quietly around the men. He soon saw why. The blankets were lying loose at their feet and the four men were leveling double-barreled shotguns at those around them.

The Pinkerton pulled back inside the passageway, but not before one of the four men noticed him.

"That's the feller we want!" he shouted. "I'm going after him!"

He pushed his way through the people on deck and charged into the hatchway after Raider. He obviously hadn't been told much about the man he was hunting, since he seemed to expect his prey to keep running. Instead he found the big man with the black mustaches waiting for him, sixgun in hand, twenty feet down the passageway. He was running with his shotgun held at hip level, two fingers inside the trigger guard, so he could trip both triggers with a jerk of his hand. The long passageway would act as an extension of the barrels, funneling the buckshot along its length, tearing up anyone caught there. All it would take was one jerk of his hand.

But he knew nothing about Raider. Not enough, anyway. He was enjoying that instant before killing: when he had the upper hand, when everything was working for him, when he could look on his victim groveling, when he could see the hopeless look of fear in his victim's eyes. At that moment the monster hardware in Raider's right hand exploded. Flame burst from the muzzle in the wake of the .44 slug. The flying lead tore into the center of the shotgun-toter's chest, canceling out the message his brain was sending to his right hand, filling all his nerves with pain, as the bullet forged through him.

When the shotgun dropped from his loosening

fingers and fell on the passageway floor, one hammer hit on the boards and discharged the right barrel. The muzzle was pointed at the outer wall, and the blast blew a round hole three feet across in it.

A small bead of perspiration rolled down Raider's forehead as he stood and watched the man he had shot flop forward.

CHAPTER FOUR

One of the three men with shotguns on deck, when he heard the shots, was all for laying waste to everyone.

"We told you not to try nothin', you goddamn sons of bitches!" he hollered. "We're gonna chop you up with this here buckshot, so's we're gonna have to shovel the pieces of you over the side for the catfish to eat!"

Seeing that he meant what he was saying, one of his partners told him, "These folks done nothin'. Go see what happened in there."

He wasn't as keen on that as he was on shooting the defenseless passengers. All any of them knew was that there had been two reports—a revolver shot, a shotgun blast, then silence. Nothing since. Had they killed each other? Or was their partner dead and the big dude with the sixgun standing there, waiting to put out the eye of the next man who poked his head through the hatchway.

"Don't none of you move a muscle!" the gunman hollered at the passengers. "If one of you moves, I don't care what anyone says to me, I'll give you all both barrels at gut level. It'd pleasure me to do it."

He went reluctantly to the hatchway, held the shotgun at arm's length inside, then discharged one barrel down the passageway. Then he thrust his head quickly inside to see what had been there.

The man Raider had nailed with a bullet in the chest, a fire of agony building inside him, half blind, half crazed, had got to his hands and knees and was crawling toward the hatchway, whimpering and drooling blood. He tried to cry out a warning when he saw the evil double eyes of the twin barrels thrust in the hatchway, staring at him. All that came from his mouth was a strangulated gasp. The blast from the gun tore off the top of his skull.

When the shooter stuck his head in to see what was in the passageway, he saw the mangled remains of his partner, the man's blood splattered on the walls and floor, but nothing else. No sign of the big man with the sixgun who they were here to kill.

They would have to find him, even if it meant searching the steamboat from one end to the other. He rejoined the two men outside. Together they herded the passengers and crew into the saloon, told them drinks were on the house, but any man who tried to come out would be shot, and locked all the doors from the outside. It was then they noticed that the *Burlington Queen* was no longer steaming downriver toward Dubuque, but cutting across the slough on another channel and heading toward the nearby town of Cassville, the lights of which where glowing in the dusk.

"The son of a bitch captain is trying to turn the law on us."

The man who had fired into the passageway tried to reach the wheelhouse but a locked heavy wood door barred his way. He broke his shotgun, pulled out the spent cartridge and replaced it with a charge

of birdshot instead of buckshot. He walked back
along the deck to a place where he had a view of the
captain and crewman in the wheelhouse through one
of its large windows. He put the shotgun to his
shoulder, discharged the birdshot, and showered the
two rivermen with tiny lead pellets and fragments of
glass. Both men were cut and bleeding. Although
neither had been seriously hurt, the incident did
make a big impression on them, especially since they
couldn't duck down for cover and steer the paddle-
wheeler at the same time.

"Kill your engines, Mr. McIhenny," the captain
called down through the speaking tube.

"Engines cut, sir," the engineer replied. It was not
for him to question the captain's order.

The thrumming pulse of the engines faltered and
stopped. The big paddlewheels on either side halted.
Everyone on board had become so used to the noise
that they no longer noticed it. Now that the engines
were silent, the quietness seemed unnatural. The
captain and wheelman ducked down out of sight.
Now that the engines were off, they had no control
anyway and no wish to have their faces shot off. The
steamboat drifted freely in the river current for a
minute before bumping gently against a sandbank.
The stern began to swing around with the current,
until it too stuck fast against a sandbank. The *Burlington Queen* now lay broadside across the current,
held fast in the shallows.

Very few of the people locked in the saloon noticed any of this. They were all throwing back free
booze and were oblivious to the trouble outside.
Most couldn't give a shit if the steamboat sailed for
Cairo, Egypt, instead of Cairo, Illinois, so long as
the liquor supply held out. A bunch of men were
outside one door. They had been elsewhere on the
ship when those on deck were rounded up and herded

into the saloon. Now they were mad as hell to find they had been locked out of the party. The three men with shotguns unlocked the door and pushed them inside, locked it once more, and then went in search of Raider, scatterguns held hip high, both hammers cocked, fingers on the triggers.

Raider knew they would come looking for him. The ship's structure—passageways, cabins, open decks— gave their shotguns the advantage over his sixgun or carbine. He saw them herd most of the passengers inside the saloon, to clear the decks so he would be easier to find..He heard the shot and the ship's engines stop, then felt the ship run aground. No one was going anywhere now. Raider decided that his best bet was to ambush the three searchers. The ship's hold would be one good place to do that—though they might expect to find him there. He moved quickly from level to level, up and down gangways, looking for other suitable places, using to the full his advantage over the three men in knowing the ship's layout.

They were confused and moved slowly, losing touch with one another as they searched. Had the steamboat been bigger, the Pinkerton could have hoped to slip past them unseen. But the *Burlington Queen* was much too small. Raider could make use of the darkness to make the searchers' job harder; he could quench the oil lamps if he chose, except that could work against him as well as for him if he too needed to see in a hurry. Also, quenching lamps would indicate his whereabouts to the three men.

Raider was a man of action, a fighter, and he thought in the ways of such men. This meant that when it came to gunfighting, he never thought to count a woman in. When Raider was adding up the odds against him, he was thinking of the three shot-gun-toting men. He totally forgot about the suppos-

edly ill woman he had helped aboard, until he met
her in a passageway looking bright-eyed, healthy,
and mean, a silver-plated pocket revolver in her
hand.

"'pon my word," she said in an easy Louisiana
drawl, "you must be the one called Raider. I thank you
for helpin' me on board. That was most gallant. This
little gun I'm holdin' is only twenty-two caliber, and I
know that might not be enough to stop a big, strong
man like you, but there's four shots and I'll put at least
three of 'em in you before you can lay a hand on me or
draw that big Colt of yours out of its holster."

"It's a Remington, ma'am."

"Whatever. You just hold it in your fingers and
drop it on the floor. I ain't a-fooling you, honey. You
give me a nervous start and my finger will twitch on
this trigger."

Raider bestowed a charming smile on her. "You
have nothing to worry from me, ma'am." He took
out his gun and dropped it at his feet. "You here for
the gold?" he asked.

"What gold?" she asked.

"Three crates of it. Ain't that what you came for?"

"I didn't know what was in the crates," she said.

"I reckon they decided not to tell you," Raider
suggested.

"You foolin' me?"

"No, ma'am. Why else do you think they'd be so
all-fired mad to lay their hands on them crates?"

"'Cause they been paid to do it," she said. "They
don't know what's in them either."

"But you do, and I do. Maybe you and me can do
some business with each other."

"What?"

Raider smiled again. " All the gold you can carry.
Though I warn you, it's kinda heavy."

"For what?"

"To put away your gun an' walk away," he said. "That ain't much to ask."

She thought about it.

Raider went on, "You see, you'd win either way. If they get me, you go along with them. If I get them, you collect as much gold as you can carry. How can you lose?"

"That wasn't what I was thinkin' about," she said coolly, making a show of keeping the gun on him. "I believe you about the gold, that makes sense. It don't make no sense that a lawman like you is going to let someone like me walk off with any of it. Don't make me no promises. I been listenin' to men make me promises since I was sixteen. Ain't a single one been kept yet. I don't need you. I have other things in mind."

Down the passageway behind her, Raider saw a cabin door open inward silently. A woman's hand holding a derringer showed from the doorway. He recognized the derringer as the one Marie had taken from Bob, his previous attacker. Marie peeped around the doorway. She was taking her time. This woman was getting set to shoot him.

He said hurriedly, "There's an important thing you don't know 'bout."

She looked at him suspiciously. "You playin' for time?"

Raider said with total sincerity, "If you knew 'bout this, you'd make a change in your plans."

Marie raised the derringer. She was more than ten feet behind the woman and wouldn't stand a chance of hitting her. The derringer was a single-shot weapon, and he had seen people miss their target with a derringer at three feet.

Raider shook his head urgently. "No. You're much too far away. You need to come closer."

"You take me for a fool?" the woman asked sharply. "I'm comin' no closer to you."

Marie tiptoed up behind her. The woman heard her steps on the floor and whirled about. Marie fired, from about six feet away.

Certain she would miss, Raider charged forward. Hoping Marie's bullet wouldn't hit him, he tried to get to the woman before she recovered enough from her surprise to start using her revolver. He was astounded to see the woman slump to the floor before he could reach her. He looked down long enough at her to see a neat bullet hole high in her forehead.

He kissed Marie's cheek. "Thanks. You go back in your cabin. They'll think I killed her."

He waited until she was back inside her cabin, then picked up his own gun and took the pocket revolver from the dead woman's hand. The men hunting him might or might not have heard the report of the small-caliber revolver. Still searching for a good point of ambush, Raider made his way cautiously through some more passageways and up and down gangways, until he met a man face to face. It was the gambler he had spent so many hours playing poker with.

"Where are you headed?" the Pinkerton asked in a tight voice, his palm brushing his gun handle.

The gambler shifted uneasily, then decided to throw in his cards. "They offered some of us a ten-dollar gold piece for the first man who spots you. I've had a bad day. I could use that ten."

"Bullshit," Raider said. "My guess is you have close to a thousand dollars in greenbacks stuffed in your boots. You're the kinda man who'll go to his grave early because you were greedy for an extra ten." He rooted with his left hand in a pocket, found two five-dollar gold pieces and handed them to the gambler. "Go to the stern of the ship in a hurry an' raise a holler back there that you just seen me."

The gambler nodded and started to move away.

"Don't mess with me," Raider called after him, "or you'll be collectin' lead instead o' gold."

The gambler raised his hands to show he had no cards concealed. Raider watched him hurry aft and disappear around a corner. A minute later he heard his shouts from well astern and climbed some steps to the main deck. He came up just forward of one paddle-wheel. Keeping to the dark areas away from lamps as best he could, he made his way forward until he saw two ropes tied to the deck rail. Peering down through the darkness, he could make out the rowboat in which the men came. It was tied on the side away from which the ship had run aground, and thus had not been crushed between the ship's side and a sandbar.

Raider had seen crewmen do it often enough. It looked easy. Checking that there was no one to see him on this part of the deck, he climbed the rail, clasped one rope with his hands and knees, then slid down it. He was a much bigger, heavier man than any he had ever seen slide down a rope. He found himself traveling downward one hell of a lot faster than he had seen them move, and the rope burned in his hands hot enough to skin his palms. He managed to hold on until his boots hit the rowboat where the two sides met to form the bow. The bow sank beneath him and the rowboat's other end pitched up. Then the bow bounced back up, and would have pitched him in the water had he not by now been entangled in the mooring rope. He stepped down into the rowboat, realizing he had been lucky to land where he did. If he had come straight down into the boat as he had planned, his boots would probably have shattered its boards and sunk it.

He cut both mooring ropes with his bowie knife and pushed away from the steamboat's side. The rowboat drifted with the current. Although he would be hard to see on the dark river, Raider wanted to put some space between him and the steamboat since he felt like a sitting duck out on the water. He put the oars in the oarlocks and grasped the splintery wood with his skinned palms. The damn things wouldn't work together for him, making the rowboat zigzag, and the oar made a loud splashing noise each time he dipped them in the water. This was another thing that looked easier than it turned out to be.

Keeping as quiet as he could, Raider headed for a nearby island, a good-sized one with tall trees visible against the night sky. The lighted hulk of the steamboat slowly got farther away from him until he felt the bottom of his rowboat grind on stones and sand at the island's edge.

He stayed where he was for a minute, looking around him. Everything was silent, except for a gurgle of water against the boat. The stars were out, but no moon. The lights on the steamboat's decks a quarter mile away made them look like the balconies of a large building. The lights of Cassville glimmered much farther in the distance. There was nothing else to be seen on the water except drawn-out rippling reflections on the big river's moving surface.

Raider woke at first light, lying on his back in the rowboat. He had found a long narrow inlet in the island the previous night and had poled the boat up it with an oar. Having heard how sudden floods can cover islands for hours on end, he had decided to sleep in the boat. No snakes could bother him either. A thick river mist blotted out everything, but he knew exactly where he was as soon as his eyes opened from sleep. He was on an island and the gold he was protecting was on a steamboat. That was the first problem he had to take care of. He felt he had made the right choice in leaving the paddlewheeler when he did—once he heard they were bribing passengers to help find him, he knew he didn't have a chance. Instead he had got himself some shuteye. He hoped the three men had spent the whole night searching for him and would be feeling a bit the worse for wear now. The gold was too heavy for them to have left with it in any of the steamboat's small boats during the night. And they would have to wait for daylight to move the steamboat off the sandbanks. The mist floated slowly in long fingers over the water. The sun would soon burn it away. He needed to get going.

He poled out of the inlet and rowed clumsily against the current. His progress upstream was slow. For a while he felt he was making no headway at all, until the mist lifted and he saw the trees of the island downstream from him for a moment. At least he thought this was the island on which he had spent the night. The mist closed in again, and his only means of guidance were the direction of the current and the bright aura in the east where the sun would burn through. But as soon as the sun baked the mist off the river, he would be left sitting in a boat, visible for a couple of miles in all directions. He rowed harder upstream, not caring about the splashes. He reckoned on getting upstream from the grounded steamboat and then drifting silently down with the current toward her.

When he figured he was well upstream of the *Burlington Queen*, he eased the rowboat up on a sandbar and rested for a while. It would do him no good drifting downriver so long as the mist was still this thick. The steamboat would be too easy to miss. Besides, he was no longer sure where it was in relation to him. He decided to stay where he was until some of the tree-covered islands became visible around him. If he could see them, he expected he could see a steamboat. And he was hoping that the rowboat was too small to be noticed.

The mist began to lift more quickly than he expected. When he spotted the *Burlington Queen,* it was so far away he had to row hard diagonally across stream to get to it before the mist completely lifted. By the time he reached the steamboat, the mist had broken into patches. He maneuvered the rowboat into one pocket of mist drifting low over the surface and got in close on the deep-water side of the grounded ship. He stepped out of the rowboat onto the back of the paddlewheel, letting the rowboat be carried off by the current. He quickly climbed the wood blades of the paddlewheel, hoping this would not be the moment they would start the engines. Climbing onto the cowling at the top, he checked that the main deck was clear, and hauled himself up.

Raider had no particular plan. He liked to jump in feet first and think on the move. The first thing that occurred to him was a check on Marie's safety. He made his way to her cabin without being seen and gave his customary double rap on the door. She opened the door only an inch until she was sure it was him, then swung it wide and threw her arms around his neck. Raider had a hard time keeping his clothes on and staying out of her bed. She didn't want to hear that he had things to do. . . .

Marie told him that search parties had been going up and down the ship for most of the night, until everyone was so weary they couldn't give a damn where Raider was. No one bothered her, except some drunks who managed to get out of the saloon and thought she might like to dance with them. Marie had no idea what had become of the dead woman.

Back on the main deck, the doors of the saloon were open. Some men still stood at the bar, talking and drinking. Most lay slumped on chairs or stretched out on the floor, sleeping it off. There were going to be some sore heads among them. It was a rare thing for Raider to walk clear-headed past a scene like this, but then he didn't often get to spend a night in a rowboat on a small island in the middle of a river. He felt virtuous.

Down in the hold, two of the brothers were guarding the crates, one awake and the other asleep. The boys told him the men with the shotguns had been down to locate the three crates but hadn't opened them. Raider checked to make sure the lids had not been tampered with and told the brothers they were doing a fine job, although he did not expect them to defend the crates, just to raise the alarm if they could do so without getting hurt. It occurred to him for the first time that their safety was threatened, but it was too late to call things off now. The three boys had a lot of pride in the job they were doing. It was up to Raider to make sure nothing happened to them.

The Pinkerton walked along the deck, no longer making any effort at concealment. He glanced up and saw the captain in the wheelhouse, looking down at the sandbars and no doubt waiting for the mist to fully lift before ordering the engines started. Three men were in the wheelhouse with him. One carried a shotgun with the barrels upturned. They didn't see him as he approached along the deck beneath them. The back window of the wheelhouse had no glass where one of them had fired the charge of birdshot through it.

Raider was looking up at the wheelhouse and only saw the movement out of the corner of his eye. Without thinking, his hand went to his gun. He drew and thumbed back the hammer as he wheeled around to face the unknown threat. His instincts proved true. One of the three sons of bitches was leveling the

double barrels of his scatter gun at him—only two of
them were with the captain in the wheelhouse, the
third man up there must be a crewman. Raider
pointed the Remington's barrel. He knew he had
him. He squeezed the trigger.

The .44 slug struck one barrel of the shotgun,
denting the steel deeply and almost knocking the
weapon from the man's grip. The bullet ricocheted
harmlessly into the air out over the river.

The man held onto the shotgun and pulled home
one trigger so he could blow away the big dude with
the sixgun. As the shotgun's hammer hit home,
Raider hadn't yet readied his second shot. There was
nowhere for him to go, caught on the open deck.

The powder at the cartridge base exploded, forcing
the buckshot in the only direction it could go—along
the barrel. But the traveling buckshot was constricted
by the dent made by the bullet in that barrel. The gas
pressure built up behind the constricted shot at an
explosive rate and ruptured the gun barrel.

The steel barrel tore apart, emptying its contents
into the face of the man holding the gun. The blast
and the buckshot, at such close quarters, scraped the
flesh off his bones, leaving half his face a clean-
picked, naked, grinning skull. The other half was a
shapeless bloody pulp.

The two in the wheelhouse were now joining the
fray, aiming their shotgun barrels out the glassless
back window of the wheelhouse. Raider wheeled on
them, sighting along the barrel of his upturned revolver. Both men, along with the captain and crewman, ducked down out of sight. The Pinkerton's
bullet knocked the high-crowned hat off the man he
had aimed at. He lowered the barrel a few feet and
aimed a shot at the plank siding of the wheelhouse,
just about where he thought his target was crouching.
The slug penetrated the wood, but Raider knew that

the impact would use up most of its power even if it did emerge on the other side.

"Hold your fire, Raider!" someone yelled from the wheelhouse. "I got something to show you."

"Be quick about it," Raider called back, taking the opportunity to replace the spent shells in his six-gun.

The captain's head appeared in the window. It was being pushed upward by a shotgun muzzle tucked in closely beneath the chin.

The voice of the concealed man yelled, "You try anything, Raider, I blow off the captain's head."

"Go ahead," Raider shouted. "He ain't no kin o' mine." The captian had never given the Pinkerton any friendly looks but they were nothing compared to the filthy look he gave him now.

"What do you want from us?" the voice called to him. This time its threatening tone was replaced by a whine.

"I ain't got nothin' personal against you two," Raider shouted, "but you ain't leavin' this boat breathin' good river air till I know who hired you."

There was a pause after this. The shotgun was removed from under the captain's chin and all four men in the wheelhouse stood to their full height, their hands raised.

One of the gunmen asked, "If we tell you who we hired on with, you'll let us go free off the ship?"

"Directly," Raider said. "You have my word on it."

"We work for Harvey Waller."

This was the same name that the man who had picked a fight at the card table had given. Raider figured that every thug working the river north of the Illinois line worked in some way for the big river boss Harvey Waller. In a way, the name was useless. Raider guessed that Waller was only supplying the gunsels to the man plotting to rob him of the gold. These two men had no information of real importance. That was why they had been hired.

Raider made them come down on deck, leaving their guns behind. He had a crewman secure a rope over the side where the ship was aground. For a moment, the two men thought he planned on hanging them and were relieved to just go over the side. Raider watched them slide expertly down the rope, not skinning their palms as he had. He shouted up to the captain to get under way, and the captain glared back at him as if to say he was the one who gave the orders here.

Once the engines started, the captain expertly maneuvered the steamboat off the sandbars and into the channel. The two men were left behind, standing in ankle-deep water on a submerged sandbar in the middle of the Mississippi.

CHAPTER FIVE

The steamboat headed downriver toward Dubuque, Iowa. The barkeeps and crewmen threw everyone out of the saloon for a few hours so they could clean up after the all-night revel. Being forced to hand out free drinks, the barkeeps had opened a couple of kegs of their cheapest, lowest-grade corn liquor that hardly deserved the name whiskey. Being free, it had tasted good enough to the passengers during the night. Now, with the light of day, some of the drawbacks of cheap, bad liquor were making themselves felt, in the form of sore heads, shaky hands, nervous conditions, and poor digestion. One man lying on the deck felt so bad, he asked someone to roll him over the side into the river—he didn't have the energy to do it himself.

After a stop at Dubuque, the steamboat passed through Menominee Slough and Deadman's Slough, and then passed the silted-up tributary river that led to Galena, famous for its lead mines, now worked out, which had supplied most of the bullets for the War Between the States. They negotiated the rapids below Bellevue and those above Clinton, and by nightfall were rounding the bend where the river headed nearly due west for almost forty miles, as far as Muscatine.

For a change, the cards were continuing to run good for Raider and he put all his concentration into the game. A man on a Pinkerton's salary couldn't afford to ignore a run of luck. Back in the Chicago main office they were moaning as usual about the monthly expenses he was claiming. Raider didn't want to win huge amounts of money gambling, he just wanted to win enough so he wouldn't have to think about money for a while.

He took time away from the game every so often to go over to talk with Marie. While he was playing, she sat and watched or she chatted with the other women. She seemed to be enjoying playing the respectable woman, taking it easy on booze and cuss words, with no more fighting. Raider did well so long as she stayed around. After she said good night and went to her cabin, his luck turned. Or maybe he started to lose his concentration, with other possibilities crowding in on his mind. Only a true gambler chooses a card game over a bed with a pretty woman in it. Raider started to lose. That made the notion of joining Marie in her cabin more attractive by the minute. He quit the game and headed for her cabin.

She unlocked the door and let him in, sending home the bolt again once he was inside. It was pitch black. He couldn't see a thing.

"You have a candle?" Raider asked.

"What for?"

He bumped around in the tiny cabin, getting his bearings. She was already back in her bunk, and he let his hand glide over her body. He felt the silky nightgown covering her, the smooth taut skin underneath it, and breathed in her perfume.

Kicking off his boots in a hurry, he hit heavily against one wall. Then his arm swept something off a table, which shattered on the floor. He cursed.

"This is turnin' out real romantic," Marie observed. She laughed.

"I ain't a goddamn cat. I can't see in the dark."

"You just ain't civilized, Raider. Put you in anything smaller than a barn, you're liable to walk through the side of it without thinkin'."

Raider joined her on the narrow bunk, and she had to struggle against him to get out of her nightgown. By the time she succeeded, her wriggling had given him a mighty hardon. He cupped her breasts in his hands and kissed her on the mouth.

As his hands roamed over her body, she writhed in pleasure beneath his touch. She slipped her body beneath his and held him tightly on top of her. Her head flung back, she thrust her body upward, pressing against him. Her legs parted.

He guided his engorged member home and felt her juicy warmth hold him. He thrust mightily into her and heard her moan with pleasure. Her hips worked violently beneath his. She gasped in ecstasy, till Raider could no longer hear the mighty throbbing of the boat's engines.

The two men in the passageway outside the cabin door snickered at the sounds of ardent lovemaking from within. They nodded, satisfied, and headed back to the saloon deck. The small, pudgy man was still there, leaning on the rail and looking out over the dark water.

"He was inside the cabin all right, sir," one of the two men told him. "He sounds a real stallion. They were having a grand old time together from what we could hear of it."

"Let the fool wear himself out," the pudgy man

snapped. He asked a passing crewman, "Where do we call in at next?"

"Muscatine, sir," the crewman said. "We should be there come first light, so long as we don't hit a sandbank. But the captain, he knows every inch of this reach of the Mississippi. You can depend on him, sir."

"That won't be for another five hours," the pudgy man said after the crewman was gone. "You two boys keep watch on that cabin, one of you at either end of the passageway. If Raider comes out, one of you delay him and the other go find me, wherever I am—in the saloon or the cargo hold—wherever. You boys stay awake and don't go away, even for a minute. I'll have someone bring a few drinks to you."

The two men nodded and left. The small pudgy man, whose name was Wilson Waller, headed for the saloon. The barkeep paid him little heed, letting him wait, knowing him as a small spender and infrequent drinker. When he finally got around to serving him, he didn't feel he owed him any friendly talk.

"What'll it be?" the barkeep asked.

"This place is kind of tame tonight, after the big blowout you had last night," Wilson Waller observed unhurriedly. "I guess drinks aren't on the house tonight like they were last night."

"You guessed right, mister."

"I preferred it the other way. People were in a better mood."

"They always are when they think they're getting something for nothing. What'll it be?"

"Open a keg of good liquor. The drinks are on me." When the barkeep looked at him in an impatient sort of way, like he was fed up with this damn fool joke, Wilson Waller reached in a pocket and emptied a handful of gold coins on the counter in front of him. "Make it better stuff than the swill you handed out last night."

The barkeep's eyes were fixed on the glittering coins. "Yes, sir," he answered, a new obsequious tone in his voice.

It didn't take long for Wilson Waller to make a boatload of new friends. He drank sparingly himself, but urged others to drink up and enjoy themselves. True to his word, he sent liquor to the two men he had put on watch at Marie's cabin door.

After an hour or so, Waller slipped away from the saloon and stopped off in his cabin before going to the ship's hold. When he got there, he found one of the brothers sitting up. The other two were lying beneath a blanket, deep in sleep.

"What do you want?" the kid demanded.

"Nothing. Just moving around. You aren't asleep."

"I have a job to do, mister. I'm on guard down here."

The pudgy man looked suitably impressed. He knew he didn't frighten the kid. No one ever saw him as a threat. For some reason he could never fathom, people often seemed to feel sorry for him. This kid only felt contemptuous.

Wilson Waller said in his mild way, "You standing guard over your brothers? They are your brothers, aren't they? I've seen you kids all over the place. I guess this is as good a place as any to sleep if you don't have a cabin. It's quiet anyway."

"I ain't here to guard my brothers. They're down here to guard stuff with me. We're going to be paid cash money for doing it."

"You're joking me."

"No, mister, I surely ain't. You see them three crates? If you was to mess with them, your life wouldn't be worth hen shit."

"Hen shit?" Waller said with raised eyebrows, an alarmed tone in his voice.

"That's what I said, mister."

Waller kept a straight face. After all, the kid was no worse than the goons he had hired so far on this journey downriver, and the kid had youth on his side.

"Well, I'm just going to settle here and eat an orange," Waller said, producing a fruit from a small canvas sack he had fetched from his cabin on the way to the hold.

The kid stared round-eyed at the orange, as Waller had guessed he would. The orange groves had spread from Florida up along the Gulf Coast to Louisiana, and well-to-do folk up north bought them as Christmas treats. They weren't hard to find in the river towns. He had bought these in Dubuque.

"What are you staring at, kid? You never see an orange before?"

"Sure I seen one."

"But you never tasted one."

"Can't say that I have," the kid replied, his tone implying that this was no big deal to him, but his eyes staring at the orange like the barkeep's eyes had fixed on the gold coins.

Waller tossed the orange to him.

The kid caught it and lost his calm. "Thanks, mister! I got to wake my brothers up!"

Waller threw each of them an orange also. One tried to bite into his like an apple.

"You have to peel them first," Waller said. "I'll show you with my own. Just do as I do. But even before that, take a swig from this bottle." He passed a small brown medicine bottle to the nearest of them. "It's so the orange's acid won't harm your gut."

The kid pulled the glass stopper and smelled the liquid inside suspiciously. "How do I know it ain't poison?"

The pudgy little man laughed. "Here, give it to me." He took a swig from the bottle and passed it back. "I wouldn't poison myself, would I?"

This satisfied the boys. Each of them drank from the bottle and then set about peeling his orange. They had barely finished eating when they were overcome with drowsiness and a strange feeling.

"The varmint pizened us," one muttered, trying unsuccessfully to keep his eyes open.

Waller covered all three with the blanket so it looked as if they were sleeping naturally. He shook his head rapidly to help clear it—he had a lot of tolerance and the tincture of laudanum would only make him feel sluggish for a short while. Taking a jimmy from his pocket, he headed for the crates.

Raider was wakened by the commotion as the steamboat came in to dock. As usual, the ship listed to one side as passengers crowded along the near rail to the wharf. He slipped out of the bunk, pulled his clothes and boots on, buckled his gunbelt, put on his hat and headed out the door, all without waking Marie. His hand dropped to his gun handle when he noticed a man at each end of the passageway, with him caught in the middle. He would have been in a tight spot if they had been gunning for him. They weren't. Only one was toting a gun, and he took off in a hurry. The other approached Raider.

"Know what port this is?" he asked Raider.

"Muscatine, I reckon."

"This is a hell of an hour to come into any town. Too early for anything to be happening, too late for anyplace to be still open. I always hate to see the first light of day."

Raider saw plainly the man was trying to delay him. He was so clumsy about it that the Pinkerton didn't even bother to respond, answering him only by pushing past him and heading in a hurry for the hold. He would have plenty of time to check down there, because the captain and crewmen usually took some time to maneuver the ship alongside the wharf and secure the mooring ropes before lowering the gangplank.

He didn't have the heart to wake the three kids sleeping under the blanket, though the Pinkerton was of the opinion that when a man is paid to keep his eyes open, he has no excuse for having them shut. But he had not hired men; he had hired boys to do a man's work. He couldn't rightly attach blame to young ones catching some shuteye. All the same, he knew by rights he should kick them awake. Instead, he looked at the crates. They appeared secure, so he hurried up on deck to see who was leaving and who was coming on board at Muscatine.

In the back of his mind, he was still uneasy about the two men in the passageway. They were a signal that something was going on. A Pinkerton operative who wanted to stay on the top side of the grass paid attention to signals.

Up on deck, he was met by a surprising sight— most of the passengers were drunk, staggering against one another, many of them looking rough after a second all-night bender on free booze. The whole damn shipfull of them seemed determined to get off at Muscatine, which was a mystery to Raider, since he could see nothing special about this river town.

He leaned on the deck rail and watched the gang-plank being lowered from the ship to the dock. Then passengers began to cross it, one by one, to the shore, some of them loaded down with bundles. A group of townsfolk stood on the dock and silently examined each new arrival. No doubt this was the chief form of entertainment in a river town, apart from gambling, whoring, drinking, and fighting.

Raider watched them closely. He had never seen so many passengers leave the ship at a town before. Since only a few were taking their possessions with them, most of them intended to return. What the hell was in a miserable little town like Muscatine, at dawn, that could make all these drunks want to go ashore?

Wilson Waller was the first man to step onto the dock. He hurried along the wharf to a group of men who were standing by a shack. All disembarking passengers would have to pass this point, and pass these men. Wilson knew one of them by sight: a big, bearded ruffian who worked for his brother Harvey. Although Harvey Waller wasn't river boss in Muscatine—his territory ended further north, at Dubuque—his men were often allowed to operate here as a courtesy from the boss who controlled these parts down to St. Louis. When Wilson had failed to deliver the goods by Dubuque, he was given this extension.

This was going to work! Wilson could almost taste that gold! When he, Wilson Waller, was sitting on top of that heap of gold bars, he'd be more important than his brother Harvey. What was a river boss, even a powerful one like Harvey, in comparison to a man who owned several times his weight in gold? From now on, Wilson was going to be the one everyone looked up to, not Harvey.

He hadn't told Harvey about the gold shipment. That had been his own private information. Normally he would have passed word along to his older brother, who would have gone about grabbing the bullion for himself with hardly a thank you. Often he treated Wilson like just another one of his hired hands.

Harvey knew his younger brother was up to something. He didn't know what and he didn't much care. Wilson calculated that Harvey would guess it was some minor scheme almost certain to turn sour, something typical of his younger brother. Harvey would supply men to him, just so Wilson couldn't complain he wasn't being treated right like a member of the family. It was true, Wilson was willing to admit, that he had been dogged by bad luck. Through no fault of his own, all his ventures went wrong, while everything his older brother did yielded profit by the bushel.

Things going wrong the way they had been so far in his dealings with the big Pinkerton son of a bitch was more of the same run of bad luck. But things had to change in his favor sooner or later. Wilson was a big believer in that. Bad luck couldn't grind a man down all his life so long as he stood on his own two feet and kept on fighting. Still, it was worrying him. Not just the bad luck part. He was thinking more about his brother's reaction. If Harvey found out— and Harvey sooner or later found out just about everything that happened on the river—if Harvey heard that Wilson had let a fortune in gold slip through his fingers without saying a word about it to his brother, there was no telling what he might do. That was part of the power Harvey held over people —they could never accurately forecast what he might do. Wilson's mouth went dry at the thought of Harvey hearing about the three crates of gold. He would look on it as if Wilson was stealing the gold out of his brother's pocket, and worse than stealing it would be to try to steal it and fail to succeed, thereby depriving both himself and Harvey of the gold. That would be unforgivable!

This was Wilson's big chance to turn things around. In the future, when people talked in respectful tones about Mr. Waller not liking this or Mr.

Waller wanting that, the Mr. Waller they'd be talking about would be him, Wilson, not goddamn Harvey. It was all happening right now, taking place here on the dock at Muscatine. Wilson Waller could see it happening right before his eyes.

As the passengers reached the group of men, they were directed inside the shack and emerged a few moments later, to wander aimlessly around until it was time to go back on board the *Burlington Queen*.

It had been a long night for Wilson Waller, but it was paying off now. After drugging the kids in the hold, he had pried the lid off the top crate with the jimmy. Inside the crate, like eggs in a nest, lay the bars of gold bedded in straw. He couldn't get at the uppermost of the other two crates until he had emptied the top one. He laid the lid loosely back on the crate and headed for the saloon, where he had some talking to do. The passengers were deep into the keg and filled with warm feelings toward him when he got there. They agreed readily enough to take one or two bars ashore for him at Muscatine, at five dollars per bar. Most of them probably expected they'd get an opportunity to make off with the gold. They didn't know who they were dealing with. Physically Wilson Waller looked harmless enough. But his mind was more vicious and quicker than most men could imagine. He watched the men come down to the hold and he remembered each man and whether he took one bar or two.

Now they were coming ashore, most of them unsteady from the night's revelry, in no condition to insist on holding onto the gold bars. Waller knew there would be a few holdouts who would stay on board, but he didn't care about them so long as the majority handed over the goods. Things were looking great. He spotted one of the two men he had put to watch Raider waving his hat urgently to him from the

deck rail. Wilson waved his own hat in reply. The
Pinkerton was too late. There wasn't much Raider
could do now, even if he did discover what was
going on...and there was a good chance he
wouldn't.

All the same, Wilson's heart skipped a beat when
he saw the black Stetson and black shirt of the Pinkerton at the deck rail. Wilson did not look directly
that way, sensing that the Pinkerton was watching
him closely.

Raider saw the pudgy man who had traveled down
from St. Paul on the *Burlington Queen* standing with
some hired guns on the wharf. From the way he
stood, he struck Raider as being the man in charge,
which surprised him, since the pudgy man was not a
domineering sort. While he was taking this in, he
was also recording the fact that the passengers were
purposefully making for a small shack next to the
hired guns. After they emerged from the shack, they
seemed to have lost their purpose and just stood
around waiting. They were like men lining up to take
a leak in an outhouse!

Raider couldn't figure it out. He didn't catch on
until a drunk on the deck only a few feet away from
him dropped something that made a heavy thump on
the deck boards. The man stooped quickly to pick it
up, but not before Raider saw that it was a gold bar.
Only then did Raider connect the three sleeping
brothers and the sudden desire of a steamboat saloon's customers to visit a shack in a remote Iowa
river town.

He moved back from the deck rail and made his
way to where crewmen were taking barrels on board
in a net hoist. For a silver dollar, he rode the empty
net back to the wharf and found himself farther along
the wharf than the shack, between it and the town.

But he couldn't hope to take the hired guns by surprise; they had all seen him in mid-air as he rode the hoist ashore. Now they were watching him, waiting to see what he was going to do.

Raider didn't keep them waiting. He began to walk toward them at an even pace. Besides the pudgy man, there were four gunslingers outside the shack, and almost certainly more inside it. Raider didn't have his carbine with him, only his sixshooter. The gunslingers had good reason to believe there was nothing much he could do about the situation, except go run and tell his story to the town marshal, and that would do him no good, because they'd already fixed that. Of course, they were counting on the Pinkerton thinking along the same lines as themselves. They saw all men controlled by one or other of two feelings: greed or fear. A man could switch back and forth between them, until one got the upper hand. In their eyes, fear of them had to quench the Pinkerton's greed for his gold. The fact that the gold didn't belong to the Pinkerton made it even less likely he'd be willing to die for it. It never occurred to them that it wasn't really the gold which Raider would be willing to fight for, but his reputation as a Pinkerton operative. That was why they were a bit puzzled and surprised by the way he was coming at them.

One man reached inside the shack and brought out a Winchester repeating rifle, levered a shell into the chamber and, in no great hurry, with easy confidence, brought the weapon to his shoulder.

Raider was about forty yards away and there was no cover on the wharf that he could reach in time. He dropped on his right knee, simultaneously whipping the heavy Remington .44 from its holster. He didn't try any fancy shooting, only aiming generally at the five men and emptying all six chambers at them as quick as he could fan back the hammer with the heel of his left hand.

Three of them dropped, including the one with the rifle. Raider stayed where he was on one knee, swinging out the chamber block, emptying the spent cartridges, lifting fresh shells, three at a time from the loops in his gunbelt, and stuffing the new shells into the empty chambers. He snapped the chamber block back in place, then twirled it and listened to it click, knowing that the new cartridges were snugly fitted and nothing was jamming the mechanism.

One of the three fallen men got to his feet and sought cover behind the shack with the others, leaving two prone figures on the dock. Raider saw one looking around the edge of the shack at him. He fired and took a piece out of the man's hat brim.

The stream of passengers from ship to shore had suddenly reversed its flow. They were falling over one another now to get back on board and replace the gold bars where they had found them.

CHAPTER SIX

Wilson Waller stood on the wharf at Muscatine and watched the *Burlington Queen* disappear in the early morning sunshine. The Pinkerton had found twenty-three gold bars in the shack, plus two he had found in the pockets of a cowhide duster worn by one of the hired guns. Those guns had been worse than useless —of the six of them against one man, two ended dead, one had fallen down in fright and pissed his pants when shot at, the other three gave up without firing a shot.

Even the passengers on the ship had reason to be ashamed of themselves. Sure they had hangovers, and sure they were ashamed at being caught red-handed stealing a man's gold bars, but it was dumb for so many of them to let one man push them around like they had let that Pinkerton. The big mustached savage had struck one man on deck across the mouth with his pistol barrel, knocking out teeth and splitting his lips, because of something the man said to him. When the injured man fell against the deck-rail for support, Raider kicked him in the gut and heaved him over the side. He was fished out of the water by some townsfolk on the wharf.

Wilson heard two shots, and word came that the Pinkerton had shot the hinges off a cabin door where someone had locked himself in with gold bars. Raider battered the door open, pistolwhipped the man, took the bars and left the man lying facedown in a pool of blood.

The gun-happy maniac strutted about the decks, waving his big revolver, almost pleading with people to give him a chance to use it on them. People could see from the look on his face how much he'd enjoy beating them to death or blowing their brains out on the deck boards, so they handed over the gold bars they had hidden. The Pinkerton wouldn't let the boat leave until he had every last bar put back in straw in those three crates, telling the captain at one point that it would be a real pleasure to leave him behind at Muscatine and steer the ship himself. The Pinkerton was a wild animal. None of them could stand up to him.

The guns Wilson had hired had all quit or died like flies. Wilson saw that he shouldn't blame himself. It had been just his bad luck to run into some kind of loco half-grizzly half-human that Allan Pinkerton had trapped somewhere in the wilderness and trained as an operative. His usual bad luck. . . .

His brother Harvey wasn't going to understand that. Wilson could hear him already, screaming that Wilson was a liar, a backstabber, a thief, a fumbler, a loser, a shame to the family, a millstone around everybody's neck, including his own and his brother's. If screaming was all Harvey might do, Wilson wouldn't have worried.

Wilson, runt of the family, jailbird, had failed again. But this time, in doing so, he had deprived his brother of a fortune by keeping his mouth closed when he should have spoken up. That was not going to be overlooked. That was not going to be forgiven. There was only one thing for it. He would have to telegraph Harvey. If he could get Harvey involved and they could still get that gold before it was delivered in New Orleans, everything would turn out well.

But Wilson had to admit one thing to himself, as he stood on shore and watched the *Burlington Queen* steam out of sight. He had failed; the Pinkerton had won.

Harvey Waller threw the telegram to his right-hand man, Tug Yager. Both were stocky men with barrel chests and large, capable hands. Tug's nose had been broken so many times it was almost flat against his face. He had cauliflower ears, and a livid scar divided his left eyebrow into two pieces. Harvey, about the same height and weight, had a face marked more by high living than combat. His jowls had an unnaturally ruddy flush and tiny blood vessels ruptured just beneath the skin of his nose. Both men were fancy dressers, with Tug always allowing his boss to outdo him in some way; with pearl buttons or a canary-yellow silk vest. Only their mother—and she was long dead—would have recognized Harvey and Wilson Waller as brothers.

Wilson had abandoned caution and spelled everything out in the long telegram to his brother from Muscatine. He told about his inside contacts at the bank in St. Paul who had sold him the schedule of the gold shipment to New Orleans and the security arrangements provided for it. He made no excuses for himself or for his failure to take the shipment. Pointing out that he was now below Harvey's territory as river boss, he had no contacts to get more help. So far as Wilson was concerned, he claimed, that gold was up for grabs all the way to New Orleans. If Harvey himself wanted to come, or if he sent Tug, that would make Wilson very happy.

"That little pissant," Harvey growled.

Tug said nothing; not because his opinion of Wilson was any different, but only because he knew better than to step between brothers.

"It makes me ashamed to be related to him," Harvey went on. "Him going to jail, like he did, broke our mother's heart. Sure, they hung my other brother, Frank, but that was for something we didn't have to be ashamed about. They hung Frank for gunfighting. His mistake was to kill a federal marshal. You have no hope of justice when you have the misfortune of being caught for that. So what does that stupid goat Wilson do? He gets caught for embezzling money at the bank where he works. Frank and me set him up in the job there so we could make a big hit some time in the future. He starts stealing small sums every day and ends up with an eighteen-month jail sentence. It nearly killed our mother at the time, and I'm sure that it hastened her death in the end. You've seen me, Tug, you've seen me try to set up jobs for the damn swindler and hypocrite, and you've seen him foul up everything I gave him."

"No one in the world could have been a kinder brother than you've been to him, Harvey," Tug said reverently.

"That's exactly how I feel, Tug. Let's finish our business here in De Soto and go down and get that gold."

De Soto, Wisconsin, was a small river town opposite where the Upper Iowa River entered the Mississippi. But no town was too small to receive Harvey Waller's attention when something there needed fixing. Harvey prided himself on being a stickler for detail and often said to Tug, "Look after the small things, and the big things will look after themselves," at which Tug always nodded in agreement.

Wilson knew to send his telegram to De Soto because Harvey had told him that he was going to go down there and settle things in person if people didn't shape up.

"I set this feller up in business years ago," Harvey told Tug. "I gave him everything he needed: cash, protection, contacts. You'd say he'd be grateful, wouldn't you? You'd expect him to treat me with a little consideration. So what does he do, now that he thinks he's firmly set up and doesn't need me any more? He sends his good stuff down to St. Louis and sends swill up to me in St. Paul."

Tug knew all this. He was the one who had delivered the first big still to Joe Kemp in De Soto, had arranged supplies of corn, and set up transportation by north-running steamboats. Tug was also the one who discovered that these days Kemp's best liquor was being sold downriver in St. Louis, instead of being sent up to St. Paul, where prices were lower. But Harvey always liked to feel that he discovered everything himself, and Tug was used to Harvey repeating back to him things he had already told Harvey.

Kemp was on time for their meeting at the Riverview Hotel. He brought along his number-one hand, Doherty, who wasn't much more than twenty but who impressed Harvey and Tug as tough and cool-headed. They ate a meal of potato soup, catfish, pork chops, greens, and a berry pie, washed down with three bottles of port wine. Kemp was full of charm and gratitude and bullshit. Harvey Waller went along with it, agreeing to go out to the still and storehouse to see for himself that he was getting the choice batches.

The four men rode out together to the still, about three miles outside town, leaving their hired guns eyeing each other on De Soto's main street. Everything looked to be in order, and Kemp could account for every barrel being distilled. It was true, he admitted, that liquor was being sent downriver to St. Louis, but that was only excess product and all of too poor quality for the St. Paul market.

"If I sent that garbage up to you," Kemp told Harvey, "then you'd have cause to say I insulted you and that I ain't thankful for what you done for me. You wouldn't want to put your name on a jug of that stuff. It ain't fit for hogs. But folks in St. Louis can't tell the difference."

They had a big laugh about that, and all four rode back to De Soto in a friendly mood. Just outside the town, Harvey suggested they go around by the south side and surprise their hired guns. Kemp didn't think much of the suggestion, but when Harvey insisted, he went along with it, as he said, out of respect for his guest. All the same, he and Doherty exchanged uncomfortable looks.

Harvey Waller reined in his horse as they passed a one-story redbrick warehouse with secure metal doors behind the levee on the southern edge of town. "Be a good place for you to store liquor before shipping," Harvey said to Kemp. "Let's take a look."

Kemp wanted to do it tomorrow, but Harvey insisted. When he found all the metal doors locked, he drew a Smith & Wesson .38 and pointed it at Doherty's head.

"Unlock the doors," Harvey ordered Doherty.

Doherty didn't move, didn't even blink.

Kemp said, "Harvey, he ain't got the keys."

"If he doesn't, it's going to cost him his life," Harvey announced like he meant what he said.

Doherty still didn't blink.

Kemp pleaded, "Harvey, what good's this doing you? What do you get by killing him?"

"I'll tell you what I get," Harvey said, aiming the revolver carefully at Doherty's head. "When I shoot him dead, I make you move your fat ass in a hurry to open those doors and quit lying to me."

Kemp glanced at Tug and saw that he was holding a pistol down by his side in case of sudden need. Kemp's shoulders sagged. He said, "Open the doors, Doherty."

Harvey relieved Doherty of his sidearm, and the man went about unlocking the doors and sliding them open as if all this meant nothing to him. Tug took Kemp's gun. Kemp tried to look surprised at the barrels stacked inside. Doherty didn't bother to try to look anything. The barrels were all stenciled with the letters StL.

Harvey selected a barrel at random. He said to Doherty, "Get some tools. Take the top off."

Kemp suggested, "We can open the bung if you want to taste it."

"Take the goddamn top off that barrel!" Harvey roared. He was working himself up, and an even brighter red flush than usual was lighting up his jowls.

When the barrel top came off, the smell of corn liquor wafted up to them. Harvey pocketed his gun and dipped his fingers in the clear liquid and tasted them. Tug followed suit.

"Top quality," Harvey judged. "Better than any stuff I've had from you in more than a year. Come here, Kemp, I want you to taste it for yourself."

Kemp was thinking hard as he walked to the barrel and saw too late the roundhouse hook Harvey threw at his midsection. The punch connected, and Kemp doubled over, gasping for air. Harvey wrenched one of Kemp's arms up behind his back and forced him to stoop over the open barrel.

"I want you to taste the quality of this St. Louis stuff, Kemp," Harvey snarled. He nodded for Doherty to take Kemp's other arm. "Make your mind up fast whose side you're on, Doherty."

Doherty twisted Kemp's other arm behind his back, and together he and Waller forced Kemp's head beneath the surface of the corn liquor. Kemp kicked violently and wrenched his shoulders, but his struggles were short-lived and he never got his head out of the liquid. When his body was limp, the two men each reached down for an ankle and stuffed him headfirst into the barrel, as the displaced liquor spilled down the barrel's sides.

While Doherty was fitting the top back on the barrel, Waller observed that he'd need to find a new man to head the operation in De Soto, now that Kemp was gone.

"When is this batch for St. Louis due to be picked up?" he asked.

"Tomorrow night," Doherty answered.

"Make sure this barrel goes with it. I want to give his friends in St. Louis a chance to pay their last respects to him."

Outside, while Doherty was closing and locking the warehouse doors, Tug Yager took Waller aside. "I was just thinking maybe your brother Wilson didn't fuck up all this on his own and have all those men killed. Maybe he really is up against someone extra mean and hard, like he claims. We could use this cold-blooded son of a bitch Doherty in going after this Pinkerton. Make Doherty earn his place before you hand over De Soto to him."

About the only people Raider was on speaking terms with by the time the *Burlington Queen* neared St. Louis were the three young brothers he had hired to guard the gold. They were pretty mad at themselves for having let the pudgy man fool them, and after they were fully awake, they hunted around for him on all the decks. But Wilson Waller had shown no desire to go back on board at Muscatine. Raider had thrown him against the side of the shack and emptied his pockets of papers.

"You anything to that Waller who's river boss above Dubuque?" the Pinkerton asked.

"A brother," Wilson admitted readily, hoping his connection would spare him from injury or worse.

"He in on this?"

"No, just me," Wilson said.

"You kill those two Pinkertons up in St. Paul?"

"That wasn't ordered. Those fellows were loco. No one asked them to do anything like that."

"Well, I'm goin' to put you in care o' the marshal o' this town, so I can pick you up after I deliver that gold. Seems the good people of St. Louis might be the best judge o' your innocence. I don't mind tellin' you, Waller, my choice'd be t' pin you alive t' this here wall with some o' them baling hooks."

The marshal put him in irons and ran the chain through a ring on the wharf. He didn't unlock the fetters until the *Burlington Queen* was well out on the river.

"Lack of evidence," the marshal said with a grin.

"I'll remember your kindness," Wilson told him and stood there looking after the boat.

The journey down to St. Louis was uneventful. Marie announced that she was going back upriver with the *Burlington Queen,* so Raider suggested that they get together again when he returned to pick up Wilson Waller in the Muscatine jail. The captain, overhearing this, informed Marie that he was not letting Raider on board any ship in his command in either the near or distant future. There was too much trouble following Raider wherever he went.

Raider paid off the three brothers when the steamboat docked at St. Louis, giving them a bonus. The two new Pinkerton operatives assigned to him came on board and introduced themselves. Both were in their early twenties. To Raider's relief, neither were office clerks just let off the leash. Gary Coyle had spent the last few months running bullion on the trains between Chicago and San Francisco. Rob Jordan had ferried payrolls to mines in the Black Hills and other parts of the Dakotas. They each had a couple of years of experience. Raider could hardly believe his luck.

"What's wrong with you fellers that don't meet the eye?" he asked. "Chicago never sends me nobody as partners except losers or crazies or, worse still, beginners. I guess somebody in the head office goofed and sent me two real live operatives. There'll be hell to pay for that mistake when Mr. Pinkerton finds out."

"I reckon if there's something wrong with us, we don't know about it," Gary said.

"Someone in Chicago has to have a low opinion o' you to send you to work with me," Raider said.

Gary was amused, but Rob was upset by this kind of talk. He said, "So far as I am concerned, it's an honor to work with you, Raider, and I'd argue with anyone who said things against you, including Mr. Pinkerton himself."

Raider was kind of embarrassed by Rob's earnest attitude. "Hell, let's get this gold stowed in the bank, so we can raise ourselves some entertainment here in St. Louis."

They hired a wagon pulled by a team of mules and some dockworkers to move the three heavy crates from the ship's hold to the bank vault. The riverboat bound for New Orleans on which they had reserved cabins was not scheduled to leave until the next day, and it had been arranged in advance for the gold to be stored overnight in the bank. The transfer of the precious metal went without a hitch. Once all the receipts were signed, Raider felt a great load of responsibility lifted off his shoulders. The air tasted sweeter, and he seemed to feel lighter on his feet.

"Time to celebrate," he said. "Let's see what this place has to offer."

It was still only afternoon, but Raider didn't allow little things like the time of day to interfere with his plans. However, things were quiet in St. Louis; the saloons were almost empty, no gambling was allowed, the whorehouses were not yet open. All around them, men were hurrying this way and that, their thoughts elsewhere, hardly aware of their surroundings. Others were working too hard or were too suspicious to say howdy to a stranger. A barkeep was surprised to find them looking for action so early in the day.

"Nothing starts here till the workday is finished," he said.

Raider said some uncomplimentary things about cities in general, and about St. Louis in particular. When a bunch of men rode into a cow town ready to celebrate and spend their money, nobody told them it was only eleven in the morning. If someplace was closed, it opened up for them. If not, they broke down the door and went in anyway. But in St. Louis, there was a time for work and a time for play. This kind of attitude rubbed Raider the wrong way, and when a thing rubbed him the wrong way he was inclined to be ornery.

When a group of carpenters, with saws, hammers, and other tools, came into one tavern, Raider informed them that they were doing a piss poor job of building the city and that out on the plains he had seen shacks hammered together by old men, women, and children that looked better than most of the buildings in St. Louis. Rob and Gary showed some signs of concern, since the seven men in the group were large, fit-looking, and muscular. But all seven of them just stared at Raider like he was from the moon. They hurriedly finished off their beers and lugged their tools out the door, clearly hoping for peace and quiet after a hard day's work rather than a fight with some gun-toting mad dog.

The bartender was furious with Raider for chasing customers out of the place, until the Pinkerton tossed him a silver dollar to shut him up.

"There's a feller who'll be here bye and bye that you won't dare open your mouth to," the bartender said. "A mean son of a bitch, big as you. They say he was a prizefighter back east, though nowadays he fights for nothing at all except for the fun of it. The odds would be against you three to one if you was to bet on yourself."

"Bareknuckle?" Raider inquired.

"Until the loser can no longer stand on his feet," the bartender confirmed.

"I'd have to have prize money," Raider said, to Rob and Gary's surprise, who thought until this moment that Raider would never consider such an offer.

The bartender said, "Fifteen to the winner, five to the loser."

Raider countered, "Make it twenty, winner takes all."

"Done," the bartender said and stretched his hand over the counter to seal the agreement with a handshake. That done, he took a bottle of premium Kentucky bourbon from a shelf, opened it and placed it before Raider. "This is on the house."

Raider smiled. "It's easy to see who you intend betting on."

This didn't stop Raider from putting the bourbon away in generous measures, to his two partners' increasing alarm.

Rob said, "I can't believe you're going to do this, Raider. Tell me, one Pinkerton to another; tell me why."

"For the money. I'm going t' bet on myself. So will you, if you got sense. There ain't no city pug who can tame me."

"I agree our salaries are nothing much, and if you stayed within allowed expenses, you'd have to live on bread and cheese in a flophouse. But are you sure this barroom brawling is fitting for a Pinkerton operative?"

"There's good money in it," Raider opined, adding, "when you win. Anyway, it beats horse-thievin', cattle rustlin', and holdin' up stages—not that St. Louis would be much of a place anyhow for them activities."

For one terrible moment, Rob believed that Raider actually did these things to augment his salary. Then it dawned on him that Raider was kidding him about rustling and so on, but not about the fight. All the same it began to sink in that the stories of Raider as a renegade Pinkerton were not just legends, as he had previously thought them to be. It was one thing to hear about his escapades second-hand, but it was quite another thing, Rob was finding out, to meet the legend in the flesh. Rob knew better than to mention anything about Pinkerton regulations. No doubt Raider, if he had ever known them, had long forgotten them.

Rob looked over at Gary, who was enjoying the good bourbon and the conversation, and plainly no longer worrying about living up to the traditions of the Pinkerton National Detective Agency. Rob kept his opinions to himself and left his whiskey untasted.

Hog McIntosh, the ex-prizefighter, turned out to be a six-footer with broad shoulders, big hands, and a big gut. His bald head made him look older than his forty-odd years. His lip curled in scorn as he looked Raider over.

"I'm gonna knock you cold, cowboy," he said. "You should've stuck to wrasslin' steers or shootin' Injuns, 'cause you ain't in my class. I ain't some campfire bully. I'm a scientific fighter. You're so dumb, you won't know what happened to you."

Raider tipped back his hat, assuming a cowpoke stance. "I've roped bull calves smarter an' meaner than you. Know what we do to 'em when we rope 'em?"

Hog's eyes took on a malevolent glint. "If someone's goin' to lose his balls here, I'll be doin' the cuttin'."

Raider shook his head sadly. "An oldtimer like you don't know when his glory days is over. But don't ask me to go easy on you, 'cause the answer is no."

Hog lunged at Raider, and the fight might have begun on the spot, except that some of the men placing bets jumped between the two men, insisting that, since everyone had not yet arrived, they should hold off a while. Hog went off to circulate among the gathering crowd in the tavern, shaking hands with men who had won stakes on him before, getting his back slapped and being told to kill the dumb bastard. Word had gotten around, and what had been an empty tavern two hours previously, now held more than two hundred men, drinking, smoking, arguing, and elbowing their way close to take a good look at each fighter.

Raider leaned against the bar, cutting back now to occasional sips on his bourbon, nonchalant, relaxed, willing to joke with anyone who cared to. Gary

Coyle was half sloshed. He had already bet a month's pay on Raider and was now acting as his manager and trainer combined. Rob Jordan didn't approve of any of this. He was not amused when a stranger told him he had a preacher's face.

Finally, all bets were laid, with the odds settling at four-to-one against Raider. An area was cleared in the middle of the tavern, fresh sawdust was strewn on the floor, oil lamps were bunched together to cast more light, and the crowd of men stood shoulder to shoulder, four and five deep, to form a big ring.

The bartender was referee. He dangled a gold watch from a chain. "Each round is five minutes, gentlemen, with a one-minute break between. You fight until there's a clear winner or until one man yields. No hitting below the belt, no head-butting or kneeing or kicking, no hitting a man while he is down. Do you understand? Shake hands and then stand apart."

He picked up a brass tray, rapped it once loudly with his knuckles and the fight was on.

Hog McIntosh assumed the prizefighter's pose, his left foot forward, his right fist held a few inches in front of his face, his left arm almost fully extended. Raider, relieved of his gunbelt, hat, and shirt, held his fists close to his body, a little above his waist. His face and chest were unguarded, but he was lighter on his feet and less rigid than his opponent.

Raider had a wary respect for the European style of "boxing," as they called it. His old partner, Doc Weatherbee, now married and retired from the Pinkertons, was a practitioner of this art. Doc didn't have the weight to land crushing blows, but Raider had seen him sorely punish men much bigger than himself through this scientific approach to fighting. Hog did have the weight and the power to wreck

Raider if the Pinkerton gave him the chance. A man Hog's size needed only to land one heavy punch true on target for the fight to be more than half over.

Raider had that power too. That was what he was counting on: knocking Hog silly and then, before his head cleared, battering him to oblivion. Also, Hog had a gut. Raider enjoyed seeing that on him. As well as fighting Raider, Hog would have to drag that around the ring.

The two men bobbed and weaved, measuring one another, neither one willing yet to chance a forceful swing. This made the onlookers impatient. They cursed at the fighters and yelled for blood.

Raider was not the kind to be swayed by crowds. Hog felt he owed it to his supporters to let them have a little action. He probed with his left, failed to connect with two straight rights, then charged ahead, hammering alternate lefts and rights. Doc Weatherbee's teaching came back to Raider now. He defended his face and chest with his arms, so that Hog's well-aimed blows only glanced off their mark. He waited until Hog came in close, then drove a solid right into Hog's face. Hog tried to duck, and the Pinkerton's knuckles connected with his forehead above his left eye.

The prizefighter's skull was rock hard. Raider almost broke his hand on the massive bone. He parried and dodged back from his opponent, flexing his fingers, opening and closing his right hand to make sure he hadn't broken any fingers and to ease the pain. Hog showed no ill effects from the head blow. Maybe there wasn't a hell of a lot happening inside his head for a blow to disturb.

They rode out the rest of the first round and all of the second without coming to serious blows. The crowd was more impatient than ever: Hog had even gone after one man who had called him an obscene name. In the third round, Raider got his chance to land a solid blow in Hog's gut. Whatever it was made of—lard or muscle—it was almost as solid as his head. Raider began to see why a man like this had a reputation as a barroom fighter. He was impossible to hurt.

Raider had some close calls as Hog failed to land some haymakers. Each time he tricked Raider to come in range, deflected his attention, and then threw everything into a widowmaking punch. Only Raider's gunfighter reflexes saved him on each occasion, and Hog was left to follow through into clean air.

The Pinkerton chopped him with short punches, looking for a vulnerable place. He found none. Hog had used up all his tricks, and Raider wasn't going to fall for any of them a second time. The fight settled down into wary circling, with few punches thrown. Raider's hope was to wear down the paunchy, older man. Hog figured that sooner or later Raider would make a mistake and walk into a haymaker. The crowd wasn't having this. As the stranger and underdog in the betting, Raider didn't give a damn what they called him, and they soon saw that. Their money was on Hog and they weren't going to win unless he made an effort. They hooted and hollered, cussed and stomped, leaned out to yell things in his ear. A few times, they tried to push him from behind, but quickly cleared away when he swung at them. Raider held back, not trying to take advantage as Hog went after rowdy members of the crowd. The more Hog did to tire himself, the happier it made Raider.

Judging by his abuse and foul mouth, one onlooker must have had a lot of cash bet on Hog and a lot of whiskey under his belt. Hog wouldn't stand for it. He said Raider should wait, and he went after the man, who tried to push back into the crowd to get away from the prizefighter. Hog pushed in after him, fists flying.

Raider heard a howl from among the heaving bodies as Hog caught up with the man. Then Hog came back into the ring. Raider heard the howl again. To his amazement, it came from Hog. The prizefighter lifted his hand to his right side and it came away stained with blood. He had been stabbed.

"All bets off!" the bartender referee called, beckoning for a chair and helping Hog into it.

Raider fetched his quality bourbon bottle from the bar and put it in Hog's right hand.

"This is a lucky break for you," Hog said to him. "Another round and you'd have been a goner."

Gary Coyle caught up with the man who had taken his and Raider's bets as he was going out the door. He tried to pretend he didn't know Gary until he felt a gun barrel in his ribs. He paid back the canceled bets in a sudden fit of remembrance.

Rob Jordan suggested they call it a night, get a good sleep and be fresh for the next day.

Steamboat Sally's was down by the docks and catered to the "river trade," which could mean anything from well-fed merchants to hungry-looking cutthroats, from traveling schoolmarms to soiled doves in French silk gowns. Steamboat Sally herself had passed on to her heavenly reward in a flu epidemic a few years back, but she was still fondly remembered for her quick temper and cruel tongue. The restaurant was now owned by New Yorkers who had never seen the place, installing as its manager a pale young man who had trained in hotel management in Switzerland. He had never in his life before had to deal with the kind of people who came into Steamboat Sally's, and he had no wish to deal with them now. He sat in his

glass-fronted office, nervously checking account
ledgers, while hard-eyed river hands ran the place
and put up with no nonsense—unless they were
tipped generously.

"Damn, this is the kinda place I been lookin' for
all along," Raider said when he set eyes on the teem-
ing throng beneath the gaslights.

Gary agreed wholeheartedly, saying it was his turn
to buy a bottle. Rob saw his notion of a good night's
sleep recede into the distance. He felt it was his duty
to stick by his two Pinkerton partners and keep them
out of trouble. He was relieved to see that Raider's
mood had greatly improved.

"I was just about to give up on St. Louis," Raider
declared, "till we found Steamboat Sally's. Come
over here, Rob, I want you to meet this lady who
told me privately she thinks you're good lookin'."

The lady in question hadn't said anything of the
sort. However, Rob was flattered and ten minutes
later bought a bottle of French champagne. Gary was
dancing up a storm with a pretty girl, so Raider felt
relieved of having to look out for them. It never occurred to him that they thought they were looking out
for him.

Raider sensed that he was being watched, and
turned quickly to meet the eyes of a handsome
woman sitting alone at a table. She looked modestly
away from his gaze, but not before letting her eyes
linger on him invitingly for a moment.

Raider picked up his bottle by the neck and
walked over to her. "Mind if I join you, ma'am?"

She waved to a seat. "You look as if you might be
more at home farther west. Am I right?"

"Yes, ma'am." He waved to a waiter, who
brought two glasses. "St. Louis is a little too much
on the civilized side for me. Course, it ain't as ruint

as New York or Chicago, but folks is gettin' that way."

She tasted the whiskey and grimaced. "I understand what you mean. I've been here ten years, and I can say that St. Louis now isn't as wild as it used to be."

Raider smiled. "You sure it's not just you gettin' quieter?"

"Certainly not. I'm much wilder now than I was ten years ago. I wanted to be, back then, but a young girl in my position didn't get much opportunity, and anyway I didn't have the nerve. Now I do."

"Glad to hear it," Raider said.

She told him her name was Alice. That was about all he learned. She had curly brown hair, friendly hazel eyes, and liked to say what was on her mind. She was dressed very respectably, and so it was hard to guess how shapely her body was, but she carried herself with a certain jaunty air, like someone well pleased with their endowments.

She wasn't telling him anything about herself, but she didn't hesitate to put direct questions to him. "What're you doing here, Raider? Wait, let me guess. You're a cattleman, on your way either to or from Kansas."

"No, ma'am, I'm a Pinkerton operative."

Her eyes sparkled with interest. "You hunting someone down?"

"Right now, only you."

She giggled, then wheedled information from him until he told her about the gold shipment headed south. After a while, she agreed to leave with him. But when he wanted to take her to a hotel, she refused.

"I'm not a one-dollar whore," she said. "Nor a five-dollar one either. I'm a respectable resident of this city, and I don't want to be seen entering a hotel at this late hour with a man who is not my husband.

Call a carriage and take me home, please."

Raider wasn't quite sure what was going on. She hadn't said yes and she hadn't said no. Was she inviting him home with her? Didn't she say something about a husband? If he had any sense, he'd bid her good night and go back inside Steamboat Sally's and find himself a more agreeable woman. But he didn't have any sense, and he liked Alice.

The carriage brought them to the outskirts of the city, where all the houses were built along roads on small plots of land, so he could hardly tell one house from another, or even one street from another. The roads were lit with gas lamps, just like in the city, but there were hedges, flowers, and grass, like in the country. Raider had never seen a place like this before. It looked strange enough out a carriage window by gaslight. By daylight, this half-city half-country place, with all the houses that looked the same, would be enough to drive a sane man mad.

They got out beneath a street lamp at a corner, and Raider paid off the driver. They walked down a road some distance. Raider guessed she did not want to draw attention to their arrival by having the carriage pull up outside her door. But they did not go to the front of a house. Instead they walked along a dark lane, past carriage houses at the bottom of long backyards. She unlocked the door of one of the carriage houses and they went inside. Raider heard two horses in the stable. They went through it into the backyard and stopped halfway to the main house.

She put a finger to her lips. "Sshh. My husband may still be awake."

Raider looked at the house. Lamps glowed in two windows. So they weren't going in. And they weren't sharing the stable with the horses. Which left the backyard. It was a mild, pleasant night, with stars. There was grass underfoot, with bushes and what might be flowers.

She lay down on the soft, spongy grass, and Raider settled himself beside her. He held her in his arms and kissed her deeply. She pressed him to her tightly, her body trembling with anticipation.

Raider reached beneath her dress and ran his hand up her smooth, bare leg. She pinned his hand between her knees and tried to hold it there, to stop it ascending farther. But his hand softly insinuated its way up between her thighs, and in a little while they loosened apart, giving up their ladylike protest. His fingertips stroked the soft skin of her inner thighs, then reached up to touch her curly bush. All her clothes were respectable on the outside. On the inside, she didn't wear any.

He lifted the front of her dress up to her waist, then fondled her cunt, which became juicy. He stroked her clit until she squirmed in abandon beneath his touch. His soft sensuous strokes drove her to such a frenzied climax that she doubled over, pressing his entire hand hard against her trembling sex. Then she fell back in the grass, gasping, and finally, when her breathing became regular, she lay still beside him.

Raider thought she had fallen asleep on the grass until he began to caress her again. She immediately responded to his touch and soon was as desperate for fulfillment and lusty as she had been before. She took his stiff pecker from his pants and dipped its swollen head between the eager lips of her sex.

He pushed deep inside her and thrust into her again and again with a quickening rhythm, as she gasped and sobbed and absorbed the fierce plunges of his manhood.

He held back until he brought her to another

shuddering climax, then released a spurt of hot jism inside her.

They were resting side by side when they heard a door open at the house. A male voice called, "Is that you, Alice?"

"Coming, dear," she called back, then whispered to Raider, "Keep still until we go inside. He has an accurate eye with a shotgun."

Raider lay in the grass until he heard the door close behind them. Then he made his way in the darkness to the carriage house. When he considered the long journey ahead of him through those empty streets that all looked alike he decided to borrow a horse. They probably didn't string up people for stealing horses in these parts anymore, so he didn't have to worry about that. And a horse could always find its own way home after he let it go, though he admitted that this maze of streets might even be too much for a horse.

He found a bridle and led one of the two nags out into the lane behind the carriage house. He rode the animal bareback in the direction from which Alice and he had come. He found the street light where they had left the hired carriage. After that, he was lost. The roads were empty, deserted, silent, except for cats.

After a great deal of aimless wandering, he spotted a solitary man on the road ahead. The man wore a top hat and fine city clothes. He was staggering a bit, like he had a load on. When he heard the sound of hooves behind him, he stopped and waved his cane, no doubt expecting a carriage for hire. When he saw the armed bareback rider in the black Stetson, his cane stopped in mid-wave.

"Good night, *amigo*," Raider said in a friendly tone. "Which way is the river?"

"River?" The man was staring at him like he couldn't believe his eyes.

"Yeah, the goddamn Mississippi. You heard it comes down this way, ain't you?"

The man pointed, then hurriedly half-ran and half-staggered along the street.

Raider shrugged. Strange place. Strange people.

CHAPTER SEVEN

Wilson Waller found a telegram waiting for him when he arrived in St. Louis. It was from his brother Harvey, to say he couldn't reach St. Louis that day and to hold the downriver boat for him until tomorrow. Wilson's first reaction was one of relief that the tone of the telegram appeared friendly. Then he began to worry about the casual-sounding request to hold the steamboat for him. Wilson had telegraphed Raider's departure time and the ship's name to Harvey. Now Harvey wasn't asking him to delay Raider and let the ship go without him; he was asking Wilson to delay one of the big riverboats down to New Orleans, like it was a wagon pulled by a pair of oxen. How in the hell was Wilson going to delay a riverboat 24 hours? He'd better find a way. Harvey was giving him a chance to redeem himself, prove he wasn't a one-hundred percent fuck up. He had better prove it.

He had tried to steal from his brother—at least that was how Harvey would see it, although he had no more legal right to the gold than Wilson. Harvey wouldn't forgive that. But he mightn't come down hard since Wilson had finally got sense and called him in at the last minute. If Harvey got the gold, things would be all right.

How was he going to stop a big riverboat for a day? Normally Harvey wouldn't trust him to make coffee. Now he was asking him to stop riverboats! Wilson supposed he should be flattered that his brother had so much faith in his abilities. But he knew that wasn't the case. Harvey was just giving him a chance to bury himself deeper. No one would be more surprised than Harvey if Wilson did manage to delay that riverboat. Wilson intended to do it. He didn't know how, but he would do it.

The *Delta Paragon* was at the dock. It had just arrived and was still unloading passengers and freight. The multiple decks of the big sternwheeler were painted brilliant white. Smoke belched from the twin stacks. He walked on board without being challenged and made his way belowdecks. Everyone was too busy with his own concerns to care about him. He descended some more levels and finally climbed down the rungs of a metal ladder. He was in the engine room.

Heat still radiated from the huge boilers and steam hissed from pipes, but the gears to the big driveshafts to the stern paddlewheel had been disconnected. However, the steam left in the system was still driving various cogs and shafts, which would turn idly until the pressure died down. Three men in engineer's overalls were busy doing something to a gauge at the fore end of the engine room. He was out of their view.

Wilson picked up a heavy screwdriver from a workbench. He had no plan, and selected the screwdriver only because he knew what it was used for. Maybe he could loosen some screws—though frankly he was scared to touch anything in case it released a hot blast of steam on him or ground him up between moving metal parts. But he was even more scared of his brother Harvey. He pressed the screwdriver between two rotating cogwheels. The steel shaft of the screwdriver snapped off many of the teeth on the wheels, and after it was ejected the second cogwheel was no longer driven by the first.

Pleased with this, Wilson grew more ambitious. He picked a major junction where three wheels intersected, each with a revolving shaft attached. He had no idea what the thing did, but it looked important. He jammed the screwdriver in. The three cogwheels seized. The shafts and wheels vibrated as the force on them built. With a clank, one shaft snapped.

Wilson decided it was time to leave. He climbed the metal ladder and paused only to use the water jug and washbasin in an empty cabin before going ashore.

Raider, Gary Coyle, and Rob Jordan stood guard as the hired men loaded the crates of gold from the bank vault onto a wagon. They walked beside the slow-moving vehicle to the docks and waited while the driver positioned his wagon beneath a hoist. The crates were lifted onto the deck of the *Delta Paragon*, and from there the men brought them to the four-bunk cabin reserved in Raider's name for the journey to New Orleans. Raider paid the men and sat back on one bunk, relieved but a little puzzled.

"Seems strange for that feller Wilson Waller's gang to give up just because Wilson is in jail in Muscatine," Raider said to Rob and Gary. "I kinda figured on us havin' trouble while the gold was on land. Why wait till we put it back on board a boat?"

Since this was the first either Rob or Gary had heard of any previous trouble, apart from the two operatives killed in St. Paul, they demanded information from Raider, but got little more than some essential facts.

Gary said, "Maybe they ain't friendly with the river boss who controls St. Louis and they're waitin' till we go downriver."

Raider nodded. "Makes sense."

"Or they're waiting for the boss man Harvey to show his face," Rob suggested.

"Could be," Raider agreed. "I think we got 'em beat if that's the case. The two brothers are still upriver and we're due to leave in an hour. They'll never catch up with us in this big powerful riverboat."

Someone knocked at the cabin door and Rob called for him to come in. It was a steward, a black man with a booming voice.

"Sorry, folks," he announced, "the *Paragon,* she ain't goin' nowhere today. Maybe tomorrow she leave. She got engine trouble."

"I spoke too soon," Raider said. "What kind of engine trouble might that be?"

"Some gears is all chewed up, sir. The engineer had to find replacement parts. It was done deliberate, I hear."

After the steward was gone, Raider said, "I guess those boys ain't done with us yet. Well, they're goin' t' have t' come in this cabin after the gold. We have t' break up our time into watches, so there's always at least one of us in here with the gold, day and night. You find that agreeable?"

Gary and Rob nodded.

Raider stood and stretched. "Well, I reckon since we're going to be here overnight, I might as well mosey back to Steamboat Sally's."

"Again!" Rob blurted out.

Raider grinned. "Nobody's forcin' you to come, Rob. We need a man here to watch this gold. Seems like you just elected yourself to first watch. You comin' with me, Gary?"

"Sure thing."

Rob was annoyed. "Hey, when are you fellows coming back?"

"We'll be back tonight," Raider promised. "Unless I get led up the garden path again."

Rob had to smile. He had seen Raider arrive at dawn on the horse. He'd had less than three hours' sleep and he was going back for more.

Steamboat Sally's was noisy and full, with the early afternoon sunlight streaming through the stained glass windows, making beams through the cigar smoke. Raider and Gary joined a fast-moving medium-stakes dice game, doing more watching than betting and just about holding their own. At sundown the dancing began. As soon as the fiddle, flute, and accordian struck up dance tunes, women started to appear, drawn to the sound like moths to a flame.

There was no sign of Alice. Her encounter with Raider the previous night must have satisfied her for a while, so she was spending the night at the fireside in home, sweet home. Raider danced, although he was not much of a dancer; in fact, he was a godawful dancer. But women didn't expect a frontier type like him to dance well. They realized he was on his best behavior when he tried not to cuss or shoot anyone.

Gloria was a contrast to Alice. She wore a tight silk dress that showed off her charms, her hair was a shade of red Raider had never seen before, her lips were painted, her eyes outlined. She took a liking to Raider and was the kind of woman who made no attempt to conceal her desires. Of course, it didn't take much pushing and shoving to get Raider to leave for a hotel. They went to the nearest place.

In the room, he slipped the straps of the silk dress from her shoulders, and the material slid down over her body to the floor. She stripped off her lacy underthings and stood naked before him. Fondling her breasts, he lifted one in the palm of his hand and ran his tongue around the nipple gently for several moments, barely touching it. Then he flicked the tip of his tongue across the nipple, which hardened and stood up. She pushed her breast into his mouth, gasping with desire, and her nipple became even harder.

Desire pulsed through her as her breasts were caressed and sucked. She took Raider's clothes off at odd moments in between. When they were both naked, she pressed her soft yielding breasts against his muscular hairy chest. His stiff dick urgently prodded against her lower belly and thighs.

Gloria dropped to her knees and took the full length of his huge cock into warm mouth and throat.

It was nearly midnight when Raider headed back to the riverboat. He looked into Steamboat Sally's in case Gary might still be there. Sure enough, he spotted him standing at one end of the bar. He had been with a woman and dropped by again, figuring that Raider would stop in. Raider guessed he was staying here because he knew that if he went back to the riverboat alone, he would have to listen to Rob's criticism and complaints.

It wasn't far from Steamboat Sally's to where the *Delta Paragon* was docked. A drizzle began to fall as the two men walked the silent, empty wharfside streets. Wet cobblestones glittered beneath the gaslights, and the hulks of warehouses loomed on either side of the narrow streets. Both men were tired and didn't have much to say to each other.

They turned the corner of the street that led to the riverboat dock and came upon three thugs beating someone on the ground with lengths of timber. The three were so involved they didn't see the two Pinkertons come up behind them. Raider poleaxed one by hammering down his fist on top of his head. The man fell senseless. Raider grabbed his three-foot length of timber and assaulted one of the other two. The man glanced down at the gun on Raider's hip, clearly surprised that its owner wasn't using it. He swung wildly at Raider with his length of wood, and when Raider ducked, he moved in fast to try to grab the Pinkerton's gun with his free hand.

Raider slammed his piece of timber down across the man's forearm and felt the wood connect solidly with bone. While the man was twisting in agony from the blow, Raider put him out of his misery with a crack on the head. The man crumpled in silence to the wet cobblestones.

Gary had drawn his .38 Smith & Wesson revolver and was holding the third attacker against a building wall. In spite of being threatened by a gun, it wasn't at Gary that this man was looking but at Raider.

He said, "You're the one who fought Hog McIntosh. I was there. I bet on you."

"Then you were one of very few who did," Raider said.

Raider pointed to the prone man they had been beating. "Who's he?"

"Some jerk we was robbin'."

"Why beat on him?"

"He had no money."

"Pick him up, asshole," Raider ordered. "Carry him down to the riverboat."

"What about my friends?" the man whined. "I can't leave them lyin' here."

"You were goin' to leave this man. They can wait. There ain't no buzzards or varmints in these parts to eat pieces off 'em, more's the pity. You hurry now, put that man over your shoulder."

"What are you goin' t' do with me?"

Raider offered, "Do what I say. Maybe I won't throw you in the river."

The thug staggered beneath the weight of his victim as he carried him over his shoulder to the riverboat. He set him down on the deck and fled down the gangway to the dock before Raider had a chance to inflict any more punishment on him. They got a good look at the beating victim for the first time beneath the riverboat's oil lamps. He was in his early twenties, with a slight build and a narrow face. He was bruised and unconscious, but at least he was breathing.

A woman rushed across the deck and sank to her knees beside the unconscious man, cradling his face in her hands. "Johnny, Johnny," she moaned, over and over. Some of the crew, on night watch, came over to see what all the commotion was about.

It took a while for Raider to find out from the pretty young woman that this was her husband of less than four months and that they were on their way to New Orleans, where he had been offered a position with a big importer. When Raider suggested he be taken to their cabin while he called a doctor, she said they had no cabin, nor any extra money with which to pay a doctor.

"I'll pay him," Raider said, "and these crewmen'll do you a favor by findin' you a cabin and sayin' nothin' 'bout it till your husband recovers."

She thanked him and the crewmen.

One of them answered, "Ain't nothin' a sailor won't do for a purty gal. And if you need tendin' while your husband is indisposed, this sailor is volunteerin' for the duty."

"He means no harm by it," Raider assured the frightened woman.

• • •

Wilson Waller did not dare approach the dock until after the *Delta Paragon* had pulled out into the river. He took out his watch and opened it. He had delayed its sailing for almost exactly 24 hours. His brother Harvey couldn't find fault with that. He had followed instructions. It was not his fault that Harvey hadn't made it in time. He had checked at the telegraph office an hour ago. There had been no messages for him. He would try again in an hour or so. In the meantime, he walked out on the dock and looked at the wake of the *Delta Paragon* as it bore the gold away downriver. He waited until the steamer was out of sight, finished his cigar, and was turning away when something familiar caught his eye. It was a much smaller craft approaching the dock from upriver. His brother Harvey emerged from the wheelhouse, put binoculars to his eyes, then waved to him. Wilson waved back.

Tug Yager was at the wheel of the boat, a 36-foot shallow-draft boat with the wheelhouse amidship, a covered area fore of that, a coal-fired boiler immediately aft and an open area toward the stern. The boiler powered a single screw. It was a fast craft, large enough not to be swamped in the big reaches of the lower river, yet small enough to be maneuverable outside the main channel.

Wilson shouted down to them. "You just missed the *Paragon* by less than a half hour. You'll easy catch her."

Harvey nodded. "We were waiting for her to pull out so we could come in and get you. Come aboard."

Wilson was relieved to be invited aboard. That meant he would get a share of the gold. Unless they were bringing him along so they could kill him.

CHAPTER EIGHT

The *Delta Paragon* was one of those riverboats fittingly called a floating palace. From a distance, it even looked like a big plantation house. Raider looked in disgust at the massive carved and gilded furniture. His boots sank into thick carpets, the way was lit by sparkling chandeliers, on the walls hung oil paintings, featuring peculiar-looking people. There were staterooms, bridal suites, saloons, dining rooms, smokerooms, even a ladies-only lounge where they sewed and gossiped and sang hymns around a piano.

The men spent their time in the saloons, drinking and gambling. The professional gamblers on the Mississippi steamers were a legend, yet Raider was surprised at the high stakes of many of the games. The higher the stakes, the easier it is for a professional with unlimited funds to clean out a player with limited funds, such as a Pinkerton operative. The professionals here were as good as Raider had ever seen, and he'd seen a whole herd of cardsharps in his time.

It was a pleasure for Raider just to watch them at

work. The ones he spotted as professionals seemed to
know the crew. In turn, the crew seemed to warn
them away from certain passengers, who perhaps had
the captain's protection or were influential people
down south. But it was open season on most passengers. The best of the professionals avoided spectacu-
lar betting clashes—personal contests to see who
would bet the most outrageous amount on his hand
—going instead for the big pots which many players
stayed in and consistently winning a large number of
them. Most of these professionals were honest, rely-
ing on their superior skills as players to help them
come out on top.

Distinct from these gamblers were the various
cheats, some very smooth and skilled, others so
clumsy they would have been shot inside ten minutes
in any Kansas cow town. One man from a famous
Louisiana family drank brandy and won large sums
in noisy play, until the captain ordered him ashore at
their first port of call. After he was gone, those who
had lost to him heard they had been playing with the
most notorious cheat on the Mississippi. Raider had
been taken in just as the others had. He had thought
the young man a high society fop on a fantastic
streak of luck that couldn't last. Gary lost the
month's pay he had originally bet on Raider—another gambler took it off him in a little more than ten
minutes. After that, he joined Raider and Rob as
non-playing observers.

The "floating palace" made it easy to forget they
were aboard a ship at all. The surroundings and ser-
vice made it more like a luxury hotel. Besides drinking and gaming, there was eating. The dinner menu
carried six different kinds of beefsteak and some
Creole dishes from the Delta, along with a big selec-
tion of the more usual fare. Breakfast, dinner, and
supper were major affairs, with dancing after supper.

All the women seemed to be escorted or part of family groups, but Raider had faith that a more accommodating sort of female would show up as the evening wore on. This was all a far cry from the sidewheeler Raider had taken from St. Paul down to St. Louis. The *Burlington Queen* had seemed splendid enough to Raider when he traveled on her, but compared to the *Delta Paragon* she was a cattleboat.

Being cabin passengers, the three Pinkertons enjoyed all the services and luxuries. Deck passengers didn't fare so well. They had to buy their food wherever the steamboat stopped and eat it off tin plates wherever they could. They had to bring their own bedding and sleep on deck; in poor weather, they were permitted to spread their bedding in any space they could find in the cargo hold. They were treated as poor white trash by the steamboat's officers and by most of the more privileged passengers.

Raider found that Johnny and his wife—her name was Martha—had been evicted from the cabin as soon as he was able to stand on his feet.

"The captain saw us come out. He claimed we didn't look to him like cabin passengers and wanted to know how come we were there. When we explained, he had our belongings thrown out on deck and the cabin door locked. He's not a very sympathetic man."

"He's a regular dictator," Martha said heatedly. "He couldn't care less whether we lived or died, and he just about said so, too."

"Well, I'm sorry our budget can't cover that cabin for you two," Raider said.

"You paid for the doctor," Johnny told him. "That's more than enough. Besides that, you and

Gary saved my life. I owe you. I repay all my debts. I'll find some way to pay you back."

"That ain't necessary," Raider mumbled, embarrassed. Gratitude made him uncomfortable. Folks were easier to handle when all they wanted to do was kill him.

The passengers seemed to care less about the one-day delay than about the *Delta Paragon* missing her chance to race another steamboat to New Orleans. Steamboat racing was all the rage, with the passengers of various craft wagering large sums on the outcome. People still talked about the famous record-breaking race between the *Natchez* and *Robert E. Lee,* back in 1870. The passengers of the *Delta Paragon* hadn't expected to set any records, only to have the pleasure and distraction of a close race with a rival steamer making all the same calls they did. When the rival steamer left on schedule a full day before they did, the passengers resigned themselves to a placid, uneventful trip, unaware of the events which lay ahead.

"You can't miss him," Wilson Waller said. "Big fellow, wide shoulders, black mustaches, black hat, black clothes, sixgun on his right hip, goes around like he doesn't give a damn for anybody. Believe him; he doesn't."

He was talking to the four hired guns on Harvey's boat. Doherty, the killer type with the cold stare who Harvey had found upriver, was at the wheel. Tug Yager leaned against the side, dragging an oily rag through a rifle barrel.

Harvey glowered at the four guns. "You fellows listening? You better be. This coyote's been playing hell with everyone we send in against him."

"And he won't be alone, like he was before St. Louis," Wilson said. "I saw him with one other Pinkerton there. My guess is there's a third, maybe a fourth. They sent two operatives to St. Paul to meet Raider. They won't send any fewer to St. Louis."

"Makes sense," Harvey confirmed.

"So don't raise a fuss in taking him, or you'll have a gun war on your hands," Wilson warned. "Be quiet. Make sure it's him. Be quick. But get to him first or he'll cut all four of you into pieces. Then go after the other two. Take care of them one by one. Find the three crates of gold: remember, three of them. Order them unloaded at Thebes and get off with them. We'll pick you up ten minutes after the *Paragon* pulls out."

"Sounds easy," one of the four guns said.

"It will be if you nail Raider," Wilson announced. "Bagging him is the key to this operation."

The four men nodded and grunted that they understood.

Doherty shouted from the wheelhouse, "There's the *Paragon* up ahead."

"Cut across the shallows and get ahead of her," Harvey ordered. "But keep to the channels. We don't want to run aground now. Wilson, you go below and stay there. I don't want to chance that Pinkerton seeing your face with a spyglass."

The main channel swung close to the eastern bank on a broad bend. By keeping about a half mile from the western bank, Harvey's shallow-draft boat cut off the big riverboat and left it far behind.

"Where's her next stop?" Harvey shouted down the companionway to Wilson.

"Grand Tower."

"All right, you men," Harvey went on. "We'll put you down at Grand Tower, board the steamer there,

then ship the gold out at Thebes. If there's a delay for
some reason, leave one man there to explain it to me.
But I don't want to hear about delays."

The men nodded and grunted again.

Clean-shaved, with combed hair, and weapons hidden, the four men walked up the gangway to the
steamer. They walked singly, showing no sign they
knew each other. All four spotted Raider indepen-
dently. They could hardly miss him. He was staring
down at all the boarding passengers, examining each
one intently. They avoided his gaze and headed for
the main saloon.

"You think the son of a bitch spotted us?" one
asked another out of the corner of his mouth at the
bar.

"He sure spent a time staring right at me."

"Sooner we do him, the better for us."

A third gun joined them at the bar without seeming to. "Everything all right? Yeah? Better not spend
time together here. Tell me, how does Harvey reckon
we'll hand him all this gold at Thebes, and not sail
on down to New Orleans with it?"

"'Cause he'd be five minutes behind us all the
way, ready to cut our livers out. He's promised us a
cut of the gold. It'll be small, but at least we'll end
up with something that way. Way you're talking,
we'd end up with a lump of lead in us instead of
gold."

"Forget I ever said anything."

They split up. Keeping in sight of one another at
all times, the four men quartered the decks, looking
for their quarry. Even though they were ticketed for a
relatively short distance, all four had paid for cabin
passage so they could have the run of the steamboat.

Raider was in a small saloon, watching the action

at a very high-stakes poker game. Two of the men waited outside, several feet apart, leaning on the rail, watching the last of the sunset on the Missouri bank. The other two went inside: one to the bar, the other to the game Raider was watching. After a spell, this man got to passing remarks about pots to Raider. The Pinkerton had his own opinions and he was not shy with them. The man bought Raider a drink. When he began to cough, Raider said they should step outside for a while to get out of the cigar and cigarette smoke, which was thick enough to make the card-players' eyes sting as they stared anxiously at what they held in their hands.

"I ain't a smoker," the man said. "Never was."

"Me neither," Raider said as they went out on deck.

By now it was dark outside. The only ones around were two men leaning on the rail, looking out into the darkness, the way people like to do on a ship. They went to the rail between the two men, breathing in the cool river air, clearing their lungs of smoke. The fourth man casually followed them out of the saloon, apparently unnoticed by Raider. It was all going down so naturally and smoothly, it seemed to the four men too good to be true, and they suspiciously glanced up and down the deck. Nobody.

At a nod from the man with Raider, he and one gun at the rail grabbed the Pinkerton's arms. The third man at the rail drove his fist into Raider's gut and, when Raider doubled over, kneed him in the face. Then all four lifted the kicking, struggling Pinkerton and tossed him over the deck rail. The four guns split up quickly and went different ways.

All that was left on the empty deck was a black Stetson.

CHAPTER NINE

Raider hit the water with a splash. The cold water cleared his head fast. He had been half dazed by the knee into his face. He held his breath as he sank beneath the surface, blew out, and sucked in a fresh lungfull when he emerged. The turbulence caused by the *Paragon's* rear-mounted paddlewheel immediately pulled him under again. When he came up for air once more, the lights of the steamboat were more than fifty yards downstream. At least he had cleared that.

His legs were weighed down by his water-filled boots and his soaked clothes hindered his movements. But Raider found he had no need to swim for his life—he was being borne along by a swift current in the main shipping channel. He had no more control over where he was going than a drifting cork. Staying afloat had to be his first concern. The swiftness of the current made it impossible for him to kick off his boots.

In the darkness, he couldn't see where the current was taking him. From what he had seen by day from the deck, he knew that at any moment he could be swept into rips and eddies which no swimmer could survive. His best chance was to make his way to the side of the current somehow, and hope he'd be swept into a backwater where he could make his way to dry land. Instead, he was caught by a rapid, dragged under, and scraped along stones on the bottom in shallow water. He managed to struggle to his feet in waist-high water, amazed to detect the shoreline close by. He peered through the darkness and saw the outlines of trees against the stars. It didn't make sense to him how he could be in mid-river one moment and be at the bank a couple of miles away in such a short time. He walked along the shore and found he was on a small island with a few pines in the middle and nothing much else.

He saw a light on what he thought must be the western bank, quite a way downriver. He had to step over driftwood logs on the island's shore. With the aid of a log, he could try to reach that light. Waiting, stranded on the island, in the hope that someone would pick him up by daylight tomorrow would cost him too much time. He still had his Remington six-gun tight in its holster. Using his gunbelt. he strapped his boots to a log, pushed it into the current, and drifted downstream clutching it. By kicking vigorously, he tried to send the log due west across the flow, hoping to hit shore somewhere near the light he had seen.

"What did you learn?"

"A steward gave me Raider's cabin number—47. Me and Jim staked it out. There's two of 'em there. One always stays inside. They been lookin' round for Raider, askin' people, but they don't suspect nothin' bad yet."

"They probably figure he's in a cabin with some woman."

"Yeah. We got to take 'em before they catch on."

"They both in the cabin now?"

"No. One is up dancin' in the main dinin' room, where they got the band. I know him."

"Better point him out to all of us. Then we'll do him."

The four guns circulated in the dining room, waiting for the Pinkerton to leave. They were watching Gary Coyle, who had no intention of leaving. He was having a good time. A good dancer, he was much in demand with the ladies. His favorite girl was from New Orleans. She was traveling with her family, and had some serious-looking brothers who gave him dirty looks, like he wasn't good enough to dance with their sister. Gary kept things very proper with her; there was no way he was going to cause offense. He danced more often with her, until finally he and she were dancing together all the time and talking between dances.

"This goddamn shit is goin' to last to midnight," one gun muttered to the others when they retired outside for a hurried conference. "After midnight, we get rid o' him—but what about the feller in the cabin? It'll be quiet then. We can't break the door down. Then tomorrow we'll be at Thebes. Waller will want that gold. How the hell are we goin' to get it if we stand here half the night?"

"Me and Willie will take him. Jim and you go down and keep an eye on cabin 47. We ain't goin' to wait for this horseshit dancin' to end. So wait for us down there. We won't be long."

Two of the men went back inside. Gary was still dancing with the New Orleans girl.

"Willie, you stand here. Follow us outside. If he tries anythin' in here, join in."

• • •

A tumbledown jetty stuck out into the water. Raider turned the log so that it jammed crosswise against the jetty supports. He unbuckled his gunbelt from around the log, freed his boots and walked neck-deep to the shore. The light came from an oil lamp in the window of a shack on stilts. Once Raider climbed out on dry land, he stayed where he was and hollered a few times, making it plain he was not skulking around or creeping up on anyone. His gun and ammo had been in the water so long that he was not sure the weapon would fire and he had no wish to run from large dogs or armed, irate householders without his boots on.

When nothing stirred in the house and no dog barked, Raider walked slowly toward it. He saw several boats turned keel upward on the grass. One of them would come in right handy now. A steep rickety stairway led up onto the house porch, also on stilts. Raider climbed it, walked a few steps across the porch and looked in the window of the room lit by the lamp. An old man and an old woman sat in easy chairs, untangling fishing line. He knocked sharply on the window. The man appeared not to hear, but the woman looked up.

"There's someone at the window," she said in the loud voice people use to speak to the hard of hearing. Raider had no trouble hearing her from the porch.

The man peered at him, maybe trying to recognize him; then he put his fishing line down and got up from the chair. He picked up a shotgun standing in one corner of the room and came to the door.

"I fell off a steamboat," Raider shouted through the closed door at him. "How can I get to the nearest town?"

"He says he fell off a steamboat," the woman repeated, "and he wants to know how to get to the nearest town."

"What'll I do with him?" the man asked.

"Why, let the poor soul in," she said, "but keep them gun barrels pointin' at him."

The man unbolted the door and Raider walked inside, dripping water onto their floor.

"Go in the other room," the woman said. "Take a blanket off the bed an' wrap yourself in it while you dry your clothes on the stove."

Raider placed his gun and gunbelt on the table, emptied a pile of gold coins onto it, along with his Pinkerton papers, then walked into the other room, followed by the old man holding the shotgun. If he had chosen to, Raider could have taken it from him with hardly any effort.

When he returned to the other room, wrapped in the blanket, the woman was frying catfish. She told him to lay his clothes around the stove. Then she said to the old man, "Put your gun down. This gentleman has more gold sittin' on that table than you and I have seen in our long lives. There's nothin' we have that would tempt him to rob us."

The old man seemed relieved to be able to put the gun in the corner again.

"What boat did you fall off of?" the woman asked.

"The *Delta Paragon.*"

"He said he fell off the *Delta Paragon*," she said loudly for the benefit of the old man, although Raider had shouted loud enough to be heard by him too.

"I saw her pass a while back," the old man said. "She'll be stoppin' at Cape Girardeau to take on that big shipment o' corn. Saw it piled up there earlier today. Nice boat, the *Paragon,* nice boat. Pity you fell off. Lot o' men end in the river these days. I see 'em pass by all the time when I'm out fishin'. I hooked a few on my lines, but I set 'em free again.

It's too much for us to start clearin' a graveyard for 'em here."

Raider was surprised at his sudden talkativeness and also at the way the old man was looking him over in a critical way.

"I was thrown from the boat," he said. "I didn't fall."

"Like most of 'em who ends in the river, I 'spect," the woman said, putting a plate of fish before him. "Eat this an' drink this glass o' moonshine with it."

Raider was pleased to oblige. He asked, "How can I get to Cape Girardeau? Is it on this side o' the river?"

"Yes, it is," she said. "But you need a boat. There ain't no road cut through hereabouts yet."

"Will you sell me a boat?" Raider asked.

"Will you sell him a boat?" she shouted.

The old man thought about it. "I might," he finally said.

A long negotiation followed. They refused $50 for a boat. When Raider offered $60, they accepted $40. He stayed only long enough to clean his gun and put on his clothes.

"You'll never catch the *Paragon* at Cape Girardeau," the old man announced. "Go down to Thebes. You'll beat her to there if you cross the river to the east bank here and take the cutoff. She has to go round the bend to get there."

"Cross the river in the dark in a rowboat?"

"I do it," the old man said, appearing to hear quite well.

"How can I find the cutoff on the far side?"

"Take any o' the channels through the swamp. Keep movin' with the flow o' the water. You'll come out just upstream of Thebes."

• • •

There were no lights on the east bank, so he had to use the old couple's oil lamp on the west bank as his only fixed point. All he had to do was row away from that light as hard as he could. He was being swept downriver as he crossed it, so that after a time the light disappeared from view. Now he had only the direction of water flow to guide him.

Clumsy with the oars, he splashed his way out into the middle of the river, which was perhaps three miles wide at this point. The midstream currents were too strong for him to row across. It was all he could do to use one oar to edge the boat to the eastern side of the current, row hard again when he hit slacker water, then go back to nudging the boat eastward in channel currents.

The sky was overcast and he couldn't see a thing, mostly because there was nothing to see all around him except flowing, twisting, deep water. He couldn't see it, but he could *hear* it. Hoarse gurgling, like a bear clearing its throat . . . huge rushes loud as waterfalls . . . then the boat suddenly picked up speed on a glass-smooth, gliding reach. . . . In a way, he was kind of glad he couldn't see some of the things he could hear out there from his small rowboat.

He saw some lights upriver. Why hadn't he seen them before? Were they on a bank or on the river? He was caught in a powerfully flowing channel, but this didn't mean he was heading straight downstream, because the channels frequently slewed from one bank toward another. A few minutes' run in an east-flowing channel was worth an hour's rowing, so long as he could free the boat from the current before it veered in another direction. The lights disoriented him. Every time he looked at them they seemed to have changed position. That was it, of course: they *were* moving. Another boat, heading in his general direction. He tried to judge its size from the lights.

Five or six of them, two high up—maybe oil lamps
on masts or rigging, the rest low down. He decided it
was a fair-sized fishing boat which might offer him a
tow if the crew saw him in time to cast him a line.
Raider's rowboat had no lights: it was invisible on
the black river. He could try shouting to them. . . .

Before he fully realized it, the lights seemed almost on top of him, much higher now, traveling at
tremendous speed. Raider was almost blinded by
lights, tiers of them. They came from the decks of a
huge riverboat, as it hurtled past him downriver no
more than thirty yards away. The steamboat had carried few lights in front. It had plowed right past his
tiny boat, not revealing its full size until it gave him
a broadside view of its gleaming oil lights.

Some passengers at one deck rail saw the man
beneath them in a small boat amid the lights reflect-
ing on the water. They waved happily to him. Life
was good.

Raider waved back. What the hell else was there
to do? His voice couldn't be heard above the ship's
engines and rushing water. He felt like a spider must
feel, looking up from the prairie grass at a buffalo.

This was a half second before the steamboat's
bow wave caught his small craft almost broadside
and would have flipped it over if Raider hadn't managed to turn his boat's prow into it. He shipped a lot
of water, and took on some more as the rowboat spun
and bobbed crazily in the turbulence caused by the
steamboat's stern paddle.

Raider was left sitting in a rowboat half filled with
water, half submerged, half floating. The water made
the boat too heavy to row, and it moved only slug-
gishly in the current. It wouldn't take much to send
the boat to the bottom like a stone. Raider moved
carefully, trying not to upset or rock the boat. He

tugged his right boot off and began to bail out water with it.

"This gives us more time, stayin' in this place so long," one gun said to the other.

At first they hadn't realized that the boat had not moved since it had come into Cape Girardeau hours before. The steamer was a smooth mover and the dance had gone on without interruption. They had just assumed that at some point the *Paragon* had pulled out and headed for Thebes, where they were expected to deliver Harvey the gold.

"It gives us a few more hours," the second gun agreed, "and I reckon we're goin' to need 'em. It's hard to get anythin' done on this damn boat with all these people around. Now if we was to get this Pinkerton on land while the boat is in port and see to it he was left behind, that would leave only one man an' a cabin door between us an' the gold."

"How do we get him on land?" the first gun asked. "You see how he wouldn't talk with me. All he wants to do is dance with that purty gal."

When the two had come back into the dining room where the dance was in progress, after the other two headed down to watch the cabin, the gunman had asked Gary to step outside and talk with him a moment about something important, very important.

"It can wait," Gary said. "It ain't as important as what I'm doin'."

"Then come over to the bar and have a quick drink with me," the gunman said. "I'll make it well worth your while."

"Talk to me tomorrow," Gary said, walked over to the girl, and started dancing again.

It wasn't at all clear to this man how they were going to get this Pinkerton on land after he had not been able to get him to cross the room.

The second gun said, "Leave it to me. When I
floor him, you come over to help him. Chase me off.
Then assist him to his feet, put his arm over your
shoulder and bring him out on deck for some air.
We'll rush him down the gangway and along the
dock a ways, so we can knife him an' slip him in the
water."

"Sounds good."

The second gun walked directly across the dance
floor to the Pinkerton, shouldering couples as he
went. When he reached Gary, he didn't say a word,
just seeming to be a clumsy drunk confused among
the moving dancers. Then he sucker-punched the
Pinkerton, coming at him out of nowhere with a vicious left uppercut. His fist caught Gary on the right
jawbone and lifted his feet off the floor. Even before
he landed on his back on the polished boards, the
Pinkerton was out like a light.

The other gun smiled at how it was going and set
out across the floor. The band played on, but the
other dancers had stopped to gawk and glare. Before
this man could reach his partner to "chase" him off,
the New Orleans girl had attacked him, raking her
long fingernails down his face.

He pushed her away forcefully from him, shouting, "Keep out o' this, you stupid cow!"

She raised a wail. "You hear what he called me?
A stupid cow! He called your sister a stupid cow.
You saw how he pushed me. Right in front of you.
You saw it with your own eyes!"

They had. Her brothers, her cousins, all the male
kinfolk looking out for her virtue and the family's
good name. They had been insulted. The family
honor had been besmirched.

They didn't wait long enough for all these things
to run through their minds, since they were slow
thinkers and liked to ruminate over things with a

chaw of tobacco before making hard decisions. They just jumped to their feet and came running, the whole mess of them, seeing which could reach the dishonorer first.

It was a dead heat between three of them, who all landed the first blows. The rest had to be satisfied with getting in a few kicks while he was lying on the floor.

The other gunman had rushed in too close to back off now. One brother had seen the two men talk.

This brother pointed. "That's his friend!"

They swarmed all over him like hounds on a rabbit caught in the open. They banged him about until he lay still and made no more sounds; then they lost interest.

A whiff of smelling salts and a glass of brandy revived Gary. But dancing was finished for the night.

CHAPTER TEN

Raider found the swamp on the east bank of the river. He felt the rowboat bump into marshy hummocks of reeds and tall grass before he could make anything out in the darkness. He followed the marsh downstream until he came to a large inlet. The flow carried him into the swamps. The inlet split into smaller channels, which in turn divided and subdivided again, only to rejoin in large stagnant ponds, where the stench of vegetable decay hung heavy in the still night air.

By now he was standing at the back of the rowboat, using one oar as a pole to propel it forward. This was necessary because there was no room to use both oars. Yet poling was not as easy as it looked. The tip of the oar tended to stick in the bottom mud, which caused Raider to almost lose his balance a number of times, but he managed to keep from falling in. He was tired of water. It would be all right with him if he never saw more than a bucketful at a time for the rest of his life. He was a horseman and a whiskey drinker. He was willing to leave water to fishes and frogs and such.

In the swamp channels, the water moved steadily. Often all he had to do was use the oar to keep his craft away from the edges and let the water do the work of carrying him downstream. He spent the remaining hours of darkness pushing his way through the marsh. As daylight broke, all he could see were reed beds and tussocks of tall grass. He began to wonder about the old man's directions. He had heard it said it was easy for a man to go into marshes like this on the Mississippi and never be seen again. He could wander for days before he lost his strength and belief in himself. But the water here was flowing—it was going somewhere, and the only logical place for it to go was back into the main river. He kept poling in.

Bushes gradually replaced the reeds and grasses, then scattered trees appeared. By full daylight, he was moving through a thick forest. In places the trees overhung the water so thickly that they made a kind of green tunnel through which the channels flowed. When the rowboat emerged on open ponds, flocks of ducks took flight and egrets flapped their white wings, almost touching the water with their tips as they flew away from the human intruder. In these fetid ponds, big bubbles of marsh gas burst at the surface. Turtles lay on stumps and tree roots, and stretched their necks to keep a watch on him. Black water snakes lay disguised as bare boughs on fallen waterlogged trees. Each time the rowboat bumped a grass hummock, a rattlesnake unwound its ticking warning. It was too far north for alligators and cottonmouths, but it was still no place for a country picnic.

A dead tree stood in the middle of one evil-smelling pond. A dozen vultures perched on its naked limbs. They took to the air, not too gracefully, to check out a possible food source. They circled slowly over Raider's head, thirty or forty feet above him. He could hear their flapping wings, and they croaked hungrily down at him, like they were pleading with him to hurry up and die. They followed him as he poled across the pond and left only when he entered a channel on the other side. When Raider saw them resume their perches on the dead tree, now well behind him, he figured he still had a chance. When vultures give up on a man, he's bound to make it. They know. Raider had had them follow him for three days at a time in the desert, and only give up on him hundreds of yards from a settlement.

Shortly after leaving this pond, the channel brought him to the open river. He could see a town not far down on the same bank, where the old man said Thebes would be. There was no sign of a big riverboat there. Had the *Delta Paragon* come and gone or was he still in time?

Although the distance to the town wasn't far, the river looked choppy and disturbed between him and it. A fresh wind was blowing from the west and rippled the surface. This made rowing a bit harder. Raider was beginning to get the knack of rowing, no longer dipping the oar blades either too deeply or not deeply enough into the water. The palms of his hands, already scorched when he slid down the rope, now had large blisters. For a man who needed a quick gun hand like he did, a tender palm on a gun handle might cost him an extra second, which in turn might cost him his life. Well, if he'd known he'd be rowing on the Mississippi, he'd have brought gloves . . . and a cork life ring. He saw a nice calm patch of water, free of ripples, and headed for that.

But once the rowboat touched the unrippled patch, it was twisted sideways off it and held trapped at its edge. Alarmed, Raider looked closely and saw that the reason this area, about a hundred yards in diame-

ter, had no ripples was because it was too violently
seething for the wind to create any on it. It was like a
glassy smooth mushroom cap, higher at its center.
Then Raider remembered the old man telling him to
watch for boils. This was a boil. It was a giant version of what happened in a boiling pan of water, a
violent upwelling from the bottom and a sinking
down all around the edges. This was where his boat
was now, at the edge. The river was trying to suck it
down.

Raider got the prow turned and rowed like hell. It
took him several minutes of desperate effort to free
the boat from the boil's fringe. Once he had done so,
the current took the small craft at speed downriver.
Looking over his shoulder, Raider spotted no fewer
than three more boils ahead. Pulling hard on one oar,
he skirted the first, then pulling hard on the other oar,
he avoided the next two.

Looking downriver from the marsh earlier, it had
seemed that Thebes was only a short distance
downriver. He could still see the town, and it looked
no farther away than before—but not any nearer either. However, up close the river had changed. He
now saw that the river narrowed to a chute and
rounded a bend before passing the town. It was at the
bend that the old man had told him to watch for the
eddy—not to go into the bend, but to take an inside
track across it. After the boils, Raider thought that
might be advice worth listening to.

But now the rowboat was bucking violently over
currents churning together as they entered the chute.
Once into the chute, the water was calm and swift as
it glided down the slope. Raider could look behind
him and see that the river at the top was higher than
at the bottom of the mile-long chute.

At the bottom, the water foamed into the bend,
where the old man said the eddy was. Raider eased

the boat over as much as he was able. On coming out of the chute, he rowed hard to keep from being swept fully into the bend. But he didn't have a steamboat's power and got taken part way in—far enough to see and hear the eddy. Only eddy was not the name for it. It was an enormous whirlpool, big enough to swallow a stagecoach and a team of six horses! The whirling hole was surrounded by an area of circling water the size of a St. Louis city block. Raider knew instinctively that if his rowboat ever got to circling, he would never free the tiny craft. He dug the oars in the water and pulled on them so hard, his eyes popped out in his head.

Sweating, red in the face, both palms bleeding on the oar handles, Raider cleared the bend and let the current take him down a narrow side channel, close to the bank, toward the town of Thebes. He swore it'd be many a year before he would ever step into a rowboat again. He longed to behold prairie grass as far as the eye could see. He looked malevolently over the side of the boat at the water beneath him— dark, swirling, evil-looking liquid—and he was too superstitious to curse out loud at it in case it got back at him.

Doherty walked into a riverside tavern in Thebes. His cold eyes looked over the dozen men inside. He saw the flood damage on the walls and smelled the damp rot of wood. He bought a bottle of the best local whiskey and ignored the unfriendly stares he was drawing from the other occupants. Doherty wasn't impressed by them. He looked them over once more, in an icy, challenging way. This was too much for one man, a big-boned, sulky hulk with a rusted Colt on his hip.

The man said, "You're givin' us kinda hard looks

for a stranger who don't have no friends in this town."

"I brung my friends in with me," Doherty told him. He paused to swallow a little whiskey. "You're right about the hard looks. Me and my friends is lookin' for hard men willin' to earn ten dollars a day."

There was total silence in the tavern after he mentioned this kind of pay.

"Doin' what?" the man asked suspiciously. "That pay ain't so generous if I have t' rob a bank t' get it."

The others laughed. It was the kind of joke they understood.

Doherty answered, "You won't be asked t' break no laws. Break some heads maybe, but no laws."

"I'm in," the man with the rusty Colt said.

Doherty picked three others, emptied the bottle into everyone's glasses, bought another, and did the same. The four men followed him outside. Doherty led them to the wharf, pointed to Harvey Waller and said, "That's our boss."

A look of approval spread over Harvey's features as he reviewed the new recruits. "Hell, if I was a steamboat captain, I wouldn't let dregs like you on board. But I guess your money is as good as anyone else's on this river. Here's what this is all about. I got four men on board the *Delta Paragon*, which stopped longer than we reckoned she would at Cape Girardeau. They tell me she's due in here in the next half hour. These four men are to unload some crates here for me. If those men and those crates are put down here, we have no problems. You pick up ten dollars each and go back to that tavern. If those crates and those men stay on board, I want you to go after them. We pay your passage, your expenses, your daily rate, for however long you are away. Doherty goes with you, and also my brother Wilson. You do what they say. Any argument?"

"When do we get paid?"

"At the end of each day."

No one had any argument with that.

The four men stood at a distance and talked among themselves. While Doherty kept an eye out for the *Paragon,* Wilson wandered along the wharf, and Tug Yager and Harvey Waller talked things over.

"The sons of bitches won't expect us to be standing here," Harvey said. "They think we'll be coming after the steamboat pulls out. I swear to God, Tug, if those scumbags try to backstab me on this, I'll gut every one of them alive."

"If they decided to run, they most likely did it at Cape Girardeau," Tug opined.

"That goddamn fool of a brother of mine depended on some agent's timetable for the steamboat without personally checking if there were going to be any changes. It's attention to details like that which make a man successful, Tug. Wilson will always be a loser. The loose ends he leaves will always unravel and choke him. But I didn't mind carrying his load for him. After all, he's family. He's my own blood."

"Blood is blood," Tug said.

"Until he starts doing stuff behind my back. That's all the gratitude he shows me, Tug. His older brother who cared for him and our mother, worked and worried so they could eat their fill and be comfortable. So what does he do to me? Speeds our mother into the grave with his stupid behavior. Then tries to steal the bread out of my mouth with this doublecrossing scheme of his to grab that gold before I even know it's there."

"It's disgraceful and a damn crying shame," Tug intoned.

"Those are the very words I would use for it, Tug.

You and I are of like minds there. I just hope those sons of bitches didn't take the gold off at Cape Girardeau. They could be on a steamboat headed back north at this very moment."

"They could be. But we can catch up with them. That gold is heavy and slow to move."

"It makes my mouth water just to think of it," Harvey admitted. He looked down the wharf at his brother, a couple of hundred yards away. "And it makes me want to kill that snake in the grass for trying to rob me of it."

Wilson saw his brother and Tug talking, and hoped he was not the subject of their conversation. He had learned a long time ago that neither Harvey nor Tug had good to say about any man, so that if they were talking about someone they were definitely not discussing his strong points. Wilson knew he wouldn't find out exactly how Harvey felt about him until his brother laid hands on that gold. Then Wilson would find out real soon. Harvey could be very generous or very mean, but rarely anything in between.

Wilson looked upriver impatiently, hoping for and yet dreading the sight of the *Delta Paragon*. With that gold unloaded on this dock, anything might happen to him. To occupy his mind, he watched a local row a boat alongside the wharf. He was probably a fisherman. Though that gun on the hip, those broad shoulders in a black shirt, looked a bit familiar. The boatman turned his face and looked up at Wilson. Wilson saw those mustaches and the look of recognition on the Pinkerton's face. Raider's right hand dropped to his gun. Wilson jumped back out of his line of sight and ran as hard as his tubby little body permitted.

"Harvey! Harvey!" he yelled as he scampered

along the pier. "He's here! My God, he's right down there in a boat!"

"Who is?" Harvey snapped, looking in contempt at his trembling, panting brother.

"Raider! The loco Pinkerton who's been killing our men and wrecking everything. He's coming in here after me!"

"Tug, take him by the arm. Go toward town. Doherty, get over here. Tell those four goons to shoot up that fellow in the boat off the dock down there. Then you come with me and take a walk toward town. If something goes wrong, I don't want him to see our faces. So far, Wilson is the only one of us that Raider knows."

"It's Raider?"

"Right. Offer the men a twenty-dollar bonus each."

Raider knew Wilson Waller had run for help. The Pinkerton was a sitting duck in a rowboat on the water and needed to be somewhere else immediately. He pulled the boat against the wharf and slipped the oars. Sacks of rice on the wharf gave him some cover. He heaved one sack onto the floorboards of the rowboat and pushed the craft out into the water, so the current bore it downstream. Then he drew his Remington .44 and hid behind the rice sacks on the wharf. He had wiped down the gun with an oily rag and dried the barrel interior, but the gun's moving parts might have been affected by their long stay in water or his cartridges might have soaked through. Raider reckoned he would soon find out, as he saw four men come running along the wharf. Some others were making for the town.

The four kept back from the wharf's edge, so they wouldn't be seen by anyone in a boat beneath it. When they were a ways along, one man took a fast look. The boat was still another thirty yards or so upriver from them. They ran this distance, then stopped, checked their pistols and looked at each other. They were only twenty yards from Raider. He knew he hadn't seen any of them before, that they were probably the sort of drifters and ne'er-do-wells that could be hired in any town to do just about anything if the price was right. One nodded to the others, and together they ran to the side of the wharf and emptied their revolvers into what they thought at a glance was a man crouching at the bottom of a rowboat. The rice burst from rents in the sack and spilled into the rowboat.

While they were firing, Raider stood and began emptying his gun at them. He brought three down with three body shots. The fourth man began to turn his revolver in Raider's direction, but the Pinkerton hit him high in the left arm before he got off a shot.

The man didn't drop his gun. He did some staggering and eyed along the piece like he was going to fire. Raider squeezed home the trigger and heard the dull snap as the hammer fell on a dud cartridge. Fast as lightning, he snapped back the hammer and squeezed off his last round. This cartridge was true. The Remington .44 kicked and the muzzle spat flame.

The slug buried itself in the gunman's lower throat at the moment his right forefinger pulled on the trigger. The hot lead cut through his windpipe and esophagus, then struck his neck between two vertebrae, knocking them apart and severing his spinal column. His head flopped down on his right shoulder, like he had a hinge in his neck. His eyes were wide open, except now one was above the other. He stood like this for several seconds, apparently waiting to see whether his bullet would hit Raider. The slug passed a few feet above the Pinkerton's head, the man's aim being affected by the impact of the bullet in his throat. Then he abandoned this ridiculous pose, which made him look like a circus freak. He fell on his front on the wharf, his head twisted around, his eyes staring up at the sky.

Raider didn't let the contortions of dying and dead men get to him anymore. For years, he used to see them in his dreams, some real, some imaginary. Now he just calmly reloaded the chambers of his Remington, worrying only about water-damaged shells.

The marshal and a posse of townsfolk, with everything from blunderbusses to hayforks, were running down to the wharf. Raider holstered his revolver and brought out his Pinkerton papers, now almost illegible and still damp.

He said to the marshal, "I want to tell you, sir, it wasn't me who started the fight with these four men."

"Sounds reasonable," the marshal said. He looked at each of the four in turn. "All dead. I know every one of them all too well. Not even their mothers are going to miss scum like them."

The first passengers off the *Delta Paragon* at Thebes were two badly beat-up men who limped and had to be helped down the gangway by crew members. Raider didn't recognize their swollen faces. When the rest of the passengers had disembarked, he went aboard. The first person he saw on deck was Rob Jordan, his fellow Pinkerton.

"Well, I made it back," Raider said triumphantly. "You can't keep a good man down."

Rob scowled at him. "Least you could've done was say you were going."

Raider stared at him. "What d'you mean?"

"Hell, Raider, we're your partners, not just some dumb kids you kick around and treat like shit. Next time you decide to take off like that, have the common courtesy of letting us know. We don't mind the extra work in covering your share. All we want is a little consideration."

Raider could not suppress a laugh. "Goddamn. Y' know I think you might have somethin' there, Rob. I'll send a message t' you next time. Anyone seen my hat?"

"Yeah, it was found on one of the decks. It's down in the cabin."

Raider nodded, turned, and headed for the saloon.

At the wharf end of town, the two beat-up men told Harvey and Wilson about the disaster at the dance.

"Everything had been going well until then," one said. "Anyway, we left two men on board. They say they can finish the job."

CHAPTER ELEVEN

Raider had a few drinks and a bite to eat as the steamboat proceeded downriver. Mutton chops flooded in brown gravy, with potatoes and green beans, washed down with beer tapped from a new barrel, did the trick. All of a sudden, he felt very weary. He'd go down to the cabin and sleep next to the gold for twelve or fourteen hours, give the two young fellows some time off, stop them bitching. It amused him that it had apparently never occurred to Rob that something might actually have happened to Raider—that he could be gotten the better of. That kind of hero worship, if that's what it was, could be flattering to a man, but wasn't much help if he happened to land in trouble. Raider had no illusions about himself as a Pinkerton. He had a better gun eye than most men, and he was faster than most. The rest was all hard work and experience; years and years of it.

He was walking down the deck, away from the saloon and toward the companionway that led to their cabin, when he stopped dead at the sight of two men approaching him. One was the man who had watched the card game with him in the small saloon, the man who had gone out on deck with him for a breath of air. The other had helped sling him over the side into the river.

They had seen Raider also and were staring at him like he was a ghost come to haunt them—no, worse than a ghost, because a ghost may rattle chains, break dishes, or make spooky noises, but he doesn't use a sixgun to settle his grievances.

The two of them went for their guns. Just seeing them was enough to overcome Raider's weariness, to bring back his fighting edge. He dove for his .44 and hauled it from its holster, thumbing back the hammer as it came. As he brought the barrel level, he saw he had already beaten both men to the draw. But that would not be enough. He would have to be fast enough to blow one slug, recock and fire again before the second man got his first shot away.

Raider fired. The bullet hit the forehead bone of the gunman and shattered his skull. Raider's thumb snapped the hammer back. The second man's Colt Peacemaker had only barely cleared its holster—its barrel was not yet raised to a firing position. Knowing he was beat, the man froze in that position, waiting for the slug to hit him.

When it didn't, he stared wonderingly at Raider and winced as his partner's body slumped to the deck.

Raider nodded toward the deck rail. Then he flicked the barrel of his gun that way a couple of times.

The hired killer looked over the edge into the river. He looked back at Raider and saw it would be no use pleading or praying. He slid his gun slowly back in its holster, pressed his hat firmly on his head, then climbed the deck rail and jumped.

Raider holstered his gun. He had been so intent on what he was doing, he only now became aware of the confusion, screams, and pandemonium that the shooting had caused aboard the *Delta Paragon*. The captain came running along the deck, clutching a big old Navy Colt. He was followed by crewmen with rifles and pistols.

"Man overboard!" one helpful type was hollering.

After looking briefly at the dead man, the captain looked behind him to the river. The man who had gone overboard was swimming strongly toward shore but was being carried downstream by the current in the main channel.

"Shall we go back for him, sir?" a crew member asked.

"Blasted murderer, certainly not!" the captain said. "If we took him on board, he might endanger the lives of more of our passengers. He's already left one dead. What are you thinking of, man?"

"Sorry, sir," the crewman said.

"Do you agree with me?" the captain asked Raider.

"A wise decision," the Pinkerton concurred.

"Besides which, we can't spare the time," the captain went on. "We'll put this body ashore at Commerce, Missouri. Have the papers ready for the town marshal," he ordered a crewman. "We don't have time to waste there. The killer escaped. Write down all that." He turned to Raider. "Did you see what he looked like?"

"Brown hair. Reg'lar lookin'."

"Excellent description." The captain turned to the crewman. "Got that? Well, let me make my apologies to the ladies over this terrible incident. Perhaps a glass of sherry all around will calm their nerves. Boys, clean up this mess."

As the captain was leaving, one of the crewmen winked at Raider and glanced at the gun on his hip.

Raider looked down. A lazy curl of gunsmoke was leaking from his holster tip.

Raider knew the captain hadn't been fooled either as to who had done the shooting. He had just taken the easy way out. After all, he was a busy man with a lot of responsibilities.

Harvey Waller gave the *Delta Paragon* a start of fifteen minutes before he ordered Tug Yager to start the boat engine and pull out of Thebes. They left the two injured men behind in Thebes to recuperate. They believed they still had two men on board the *Paragon*. The marshal had not associated Harvey and the others in any way with the four men who had been shot on the wharf, but Harvey ordered Doherty to keep out of sight belowdecks until they were out on the river, just in case someone from the tavern connected him with the incident.

"You see for yourself now what this Raider is like," Wilson said to his brother with a certain amount of satisfaction.

"They were nothing but river rats," Harvey said. "Killing them was no major thing."

"There was *four* of them," Wilson insisted. "You show me any gunfighter that can blast four armed men at a time and I'll show you a very dangerous man."

Harvey could not argue with that. "I'm not underestimating him, Wilson. What he does, he does real well. Better than me. I'm not going to go gun on gun with him. I won't give him a chance to be comfortable against me. We aren't going to take the fight to him on his terms. That's where you were going wrong since St. Louis. No, from now on we'll be fighting him on our terms—the way we're comfortable with."

"What way is that?" Tug inquired.

Harvey grinned. "I dunno. Give me a chance to think."

Tug took the boat out into the main channel and headed downstream at moderate speed. They could see the big steamboat in the distance ahead of them. They decided they would hang back like this until Harvey got one of his ideas.

"You can come up now, Doherty," Tug yelled.

Doherty emerged and looked back at Thebes with a sour expression. "At least we didn't waste no cash money on payin' those four losers."

Harvey gave him an approving look. "That's a sound, sensible way to see the situation."

Doherty stood staring out over the side. He often stood motionless, staring at an object, for long periods of time. The others found this spooky at first. Now they were getting used to it.

Suddenly Doherty elbowed Tug and pointed. "What's that in the water?"

Tug eased the throttle and spun the wheel to bring the boat nearer.

It was a man floating facedown, being carried along in the strong current. The body spun in a rip of water. They saw its face.

"It's Willie," Harvey said. "That goddamn side-winding bastard Raider did him in. You can bet he got both of them. We don't have anyone on the *Paragon* now. It's us four against the three Pinkertons."

Below Cairo, Illinois, the Ohio River joined the Mississippi. All the passengers crowded to the rail to see the Ohio's pink water on the Kentucky side, and the Mississippi's gravy-brown water on the Missouri side. A razor-sharp line divided the pink from the brown water. Below Wickliffe, the Kentucky bluffs flattened into a dreary bogland, with trees and black mud everywhere.

The steamboat stopped in Hickman, which had the only hill for many miles of desolate flatness, and took on a load of tobacco. Between New Madrid and Tiptonville, the *Paragon* crossed several enormous boils. Raider was fascinated to feel the huge steamboat shudder and slew from the great power of the water upwelling beneath. These boils would have thrown his little rowboat into the air!

Just before the towns of Berfield and Tomato, the west bank became Arkansas, his home state. Raider had been brought up on a farm far from the Mississippi. In fact, he had never seen the Mississippi while he was still a kid in Arkansas. So this landscape didn't remind him of home, except for the name Arkansas. He had begun to notice how Southern things were becoming on the river. The towns here were Southern towns, and the passengers who came on the steamboat talked like they do in the South.

Though he no longer had any sentimental feelings for those old days, being in the South once more put Raider in a good mood. A big help in cheering him up also was the fact that Kentucky was on the east bank and the quality of bourbon available had greatly improved. Gary Coyle had himself a good time every chance he got. Even Rob Jordan was mellowing a bit, although he would probably have said he was being corrupted. The river got bigger and stronger by the hour as they moved south. They seemed to have left Wilson Waller far behind. But Raider had thought that once before, and he had been wrong. He did not relax his vigilance now, and he scrutinized every man who boarded the *Paragon* at every little river town, day and night.

This didn't mean he didn't find time for some gambling and dancing and drinking. The stakes were mostly too high, so he did more watching than playing. Gary was still infatuated with the New Orleans girl and had no interest in the kind of women Raider sought. Any sign of family around a woman was enough to chase Raider off. It killed him to sit and make polite conversation—even if he did expect it helped him bed the lady in question. There was always another pretty girl somewhere who didn't have her mother or crochety aunt or suspicious brother along.

Raider was surprised that Rob had taken to ladies of easy virtue. He would have thought it would have been Gary. Still, Gary was having himself a good time, and Rob was complaining a lot of the time. Raider went his way. He let them go theirs.

A kind of gambling frenzy seized many of the men on board, and when they won or lost, there was nowhere for them to go since they were stuck on board the steamboat. So they kept on playing. One hour's winner was the next hour's loser. Only the professionals won nearly all the time, though they, too, were subject to bad runs of luck—at least the honest ones were—when they weren't putting on a show to lure suckers in. Even away from the gaming tables, men played games of chance for high stakes. Matching coins was a popular pastime. A man might slap his hand on the saloon counter and say "Ten times for twenty" or "Five times for ten," by which he meant he would match coins with anyone ten times for twenty dollars a time or five times for ten dollars a time.

Some folks who had started out being respectable enough at St. Louis had loosened up with the dancing and the Kentucky Bourbon. Others kept strictly to themselves and pursed their mouths at any sign of revelry. But the luxury of carpets, chandeliers, and soft chairs got to nearly everyone, and they let themselves go. There were no neighbors, cousins, or clergy here to stand in judgment of them. Folks straitlaced at home went astray on the river.

She said she was traveling alone and needed to be careful of strange men. She was willing enough to dance with Raider and talk with him, but would not go to his cabin or take him to hers. She drank no hard liquor and frowned at cusswords. All the same, she struck Raider as lively and raring to go.

Kathleen was tall for a woman, almost five feet ten. She was slender, long-legged, with fine-boned, long-fingered hands. Her blue eyes had a mocking look, and she liked to toss her brown curls and turn her back on people. This was fine with Raider when she did it with him; he liked looking at her ass. She blushed when she noticed him doing it.

On a windless night, while the riverboat went slowly and cautiously downriver, passing occasional lights on the banks and even more often passing other lighted craft, Raider and she went walking on the decks. On an empty upper deck, they embraced and kissed for a while at the rail. Then Raider persuaded her to recline on a heap of sailcloth, out of sight in a dark corner. It wasn't as comfortable as a bed, but it sure as hell was better than the hard boards of the deck.

Raider kissed her mouth and neck as he softly fondled her body through her gown. She began to resist him less, her breathing became heavy, and she pressed her body against his. She might have been unwilling before this, but she was no innocent maiden. Her lusty woman's appetite for sensual touching overcame her worries that they might be seen by other passengers or crewmen. Abandoning all caution, she surrendered to satisfying her senses.

His hands traveled over her breasts, could almost encircle her narrow waist, followed the contours of her shapely ass and thighs—all with the fabric of her gown between his touch and her skin. She couldn't stand it any longer, anymore than he could, and she raised a leg so that her hemline fell above her knees, revealing her bare thighs. He stroked her legs. His exploring fingers discovered no interference in reaching her juicy sex. He softly worked her into a delirium of desire, panting and sobbing for his cock to soothe her burning need.

She parted her legs and he, after quickly dropping his gunbelt completely and his pants to half-mast, guided the head of his stiff dick between the lips of her sex. She was tight; not a virgin, but as if she hadn't had a man in a long time. He leaned slowly down on her, pushing his cock into her innermost depths. She gasped and moaned, squeezing warmly on his shaft.

When he had slid in all the way to the hilt, she gripped him around the waist with her legs and her hips began to move rhythmically.

Raider felt the wild animal pulse of her body and he thrust savagely onward to meet it.

CHAPTER TWELVE

The *Delta Paragon* pulled up to the levee at New Orleans, and the usual crowd of riverside no-goods drifted in to look for easy pickings. Raider and Rob Jordan stayed aboard, while Gary Coyle went ashore to hire a team and wagon, along with workers, to take the three crates of gold to the Alphonse Banking Trust. He found a sturdy wagon with six strong horses and then hired eight men to move the crates. Nearly all the passengers had left the riverboat with their belongings by the time they started hoisting the gold over the side onto the wagon.

Raider watched the whole thing from the deck rail, cradling his Winchester carbine in his right arm. His eyes were sharp as a hawk's and they missed nothing. They saw nothing out of the ordinary either, because there was nothing to see. The men were doing their job. There were no strangers hanging about. They had all left with the passengers. No one was watching them from a distance. Raider was watching everything from aboard the ship. Rob and Gary were guarding the gold on the land. Raider had managed this job of unloading on his own in St.

Louis. He figured there was no great call to worry now that he had two partners along with him. Though he was not counting the job as being done until those three crates were in the vault of the Alphonse Banking Trust, the gold bars counted, and a signed receipt in his hand. Not until then.

The third and last crate was being hoisted down by the crane when Raider headed ashore. He walked along the deck toward the gangplank and watched as the crate hit the wagon bed and was disconnected from the hoist. Rob stood close to the man signaling the hoist operator with hand signs. Raider saw this man suddenly lash out and knock Rob to the ground. The man was driving his boot into Rob's gut when a bullet from Raider's carbine caught him between the shoulderblades. He collapsed on top of Rob, and it was nearly a minute before the downed Pinkerton climbed to his feet again.

A lot happened in that minute. The wagon driver whipped his horses and tried to run Gary down. Gary stood his ground rather than let him get away. He aimed over the heads of the advancing draft horses and fired three shots at the driver. The Pinkerton operative would have been ground into the dirt by the large metal-shod hooves had not the lead pair of the team swerved aside to avoid him, in the instinctive way that horses refuse to trample human beings. The lead animals dragged the other two pairs sideways with them, causing the wagon to jerk sharply, knocking the driver backward off his seat, saving his life from Gary's bullet which he had aimed over the horses' heads and from a deadeye shot of Raider's, aimed, with the carbine steadied on the deck rail, at the base of the driver's neck. The man lost his hat but not his life.

The horses bolted and pulled the wagon at a gallop along the narrow street leading away from the docks. The other six workers Gary had hired, who all had pulled concealed pistols, saw there was no need for further fight and fled into alleyways and other streets.

Gary was halting an open coach pulled by two fine mares, waving his revolver in the face of an impeccably dressed elderly gentleman who, in spite of his finery, showed he was willing to put up a fight. Raider charged up and tumbled into the coach alongside Gary and its owner. In his present mood, Raider was not a man to argue with. He seized the whip and reins, bellowed at the mares and took off down the narrow street after the wagon.

Raider could see it ahead. The well-sprung coach, light and big-wheeled, gained easily on the unwieldy wagon pulled by the team of heavy draft horses. The wagon driver was back on his seat, whipping and cussing the animals, looking back over his shoulder at them every few seconds. Raider drove the mares expertly, getting every bit of speed possible from them without having to force or threaten them.

The coach's owner was not so cooperative. When he first tried to grab the reins from Raider's hands, the big Pinkerton swatted him like he would a deer fly. The wallop might have scattered the gentleman's brains, because a few moments later he had produced a pearl-handled miniature pistol and started firing it in the air. He wasn't trying to hit either of the Pinkertons, only shooting over the rooftops and screaming like a stuck pig.

Gary took the gun from him and helped quiet the screaming by belting him in the mouth. Raider drove the coach through an intersection. From a side street, a man ran out in front of the horses. He managed to catch the rein of the animal nearest him and he hung onto it with his full weight. He was lifted off his feet by the horses' speed, but he kept his hold on the rein, and the mares began to slow their pace.

Raider went for his sixgun, determined to blow away this interfering parasite. Just in time, he noticed the man's uniform and didn't squeeze the trigger. The horses were slowed to a trot, then to a walk. Five more uniformed men clambered over the coach, with guns and nightsticks, rescuing its owner, who was by now too hysterical to speak.

"Goddamn city scavengers!" Raider yelled. "Cobblestone coyotes! Policemen! Dang varmints!"

This approach didn't take Raider too far with them. He pointed out the wagon disappearing in the distance. He pleaded with them to ride with him— some of them, at least. He even threatened to shoot them. But he finally had to show them his Pinkerton identification papers and give them a short explanation.

The coach owner had by now sufficiently recovered to babble about a shooting, so of course the police insisted on returning to the docks, where sure enough they found another Pinkerton and a dead man, shot in the back.

More police arrived. The senior one told Raider, "Even if what you say is all true, and you are backed up by witnesses, you'll have to make a full statement to the authorities on this man's death."

Another added ominously, "A lot of papers have to be filled out."

When Raider heard that, it finally sank in that, after all his efforts, he had lost every single bar of the gold.

Sergeant Delahanty led Raider down a pretty street in Frenchtown, the part of New Orleans where the Creole aristocracy had once lived and which was now seeing harder times. He stopped outside a wrought-iron gate and rang a brass bell. Raider looked at the house, with its balconies of decorative ironwork, its high garden wall, the flowering trees, bushes, and creepers in a blazing colorful tangle everywhere. For a man used to greasewood and mesquite, there was something decadent about all this.

"You sure this is his place?" Raider asked the sergeant.

The policeman grinned. "Don't let them flowers fool you. Old Armand Didier was born up the swampiest end of a bayou and he's meaner than a big bull gator."

Two rough-looking men came to the gate and stared at the uniformed sergeant for a full minute before one of them slowly unlocked the gate and beckoned them in. Not a word was spoken.

A porch opened onto the shaded courtyard garden. A husky grey-haired man in his sixties sat at a table alone on the porch, a nearly empty bottle of red wine and a glass before him. He waved to seats on either side of him and pointed the bottle out to one of his men.

"This feller here is a Pinkerton name o' Raider," the sergeant said. "He's been robbed of a big shipment o' gold."

"Ain't my boys," the grey-haired man said quickly in a strong Cajun accent.

"We know that, Mr. Didier," Raider put in. "That's why I thought you might be int'rested. Y' see, a man called Harvey Waller done it—he brought his gang down here. Now, I figure that since New Orleans is your territory and Harvey Waller belongs way upriver near St. Paul, he should be payin' you a cut on what he takes down here."

"I know who Waller is," Armand Didier said. "What's in this for you?"

"Well, I reckon I ain't got much hope in you

handin' the gold back to me," Raider said goodhu-
moredly, accepting a glass of red wine from the new
bottle, taking a mouthful of it and spitting it out.
"Horse piss!"

Armand Didier looked offended.

"Nothing personal," the sergeant said easily. "My
guess is this man's a whiskey drinker."

"He drinks red wine with me," the Cajun said an-
grily, "or he drinks water."

"I don't recommend the water here," the sergeant
said to Raider.

The Pinkerton ignored these last comments.
"What do I get out o' this? I'll settle for Harvey
Waller's balls nailed to a door."

The man stood bound against a pillar in a warehouse
basement. A lighted oil lamp was set on a nearby
packing case, its glow dim in the cavernous darkness. Four men approached, two carrying lamps. The
man bound to the pillar glared at them defiantly. The
four men greeted him in a friendly way, until one
produced a long, narrow-bladed knife. He held the
blade point a few inches from the bound man's face
and slowly prodded around his eyes. Beads of blood
formed on some of the punctures. The bound man
held his head rigid, no expression on his face, his
eyes staring straight ahead, trying not to blink as the
blade moved.

One of the other men spoke finally, in a low
voice, in French dialect. "So, Jean, you're working
now for upriver Englishmen? We're Frenchmen like
you. We don't work with Englishmen. Working for
them here, in the place of your birth? We hadn't expected to find a traitor in you, Jean."

"Me, a traitor? *Mais non*. Never. A man offered
us a job to unload some crates. True, he was an Englishman, but what do I care, if his money is good?

He told us to bring a gun each but to keep it hidden. He said there'd be trouble and that's why he was paying twenty dollars to each man for a few hours of work. When a man pays that kind of money, he's not expecting to be asked questions. I didn't go out of my way to find work from someone not connected with Mr. Didier. I just assumed he was all right with you people or he wouldn't be on the docks hiring hands so openly."

"What did he ask you and the others to do, Jean?"

"Just stand around with a wagon and team when the *Delta Paragon* came in to berth. And chase off anyone else, so we made sure we were the ones hired. We couldn't chase everyone off, like he wanted, so we put out word that no one was to take our job. That's how you heard it was me and the others, wasn't it?"

"It doesn't matter how we heard, Jean. Who drove the wagon and where did he take it?"

"Jacques du Pres. You know Jacques. We all scattered after he took off and we went later to his house in Storyville to collect our pay. He wasn't there, but his wife paid us. She said Jacques would be away for a few days. But it's no good you asking her, Jacques don't tell her a thing."

The man with the knife tore Jean's shirt down the front with his free hand, then tore the strips aside. Jean's paunch bulged out over his belt buckle.

The knife wielder spoke for the first time. "Not telling us something you know is just as bad as telling us lies," he said in a sad voice like that of a priest in the confessional. He traced a curve with the razor edge of the blade across Jean's paunch. A thin red line of parted skin marked the trail of the knife's blade. "It'd take you more than a day to die here with your guts spilled out over your feet, Jean. Tell us what we want to know. Where are those crates now?"

Jean tried to keep a brave front, but he had to swallow several times before he could make words come. "I don't know. Jacques du Pres works for you. I've loaded goods onto his wagon before. He stores them for you—I don't know where. In a warehouse up the river, I think someone once said. But I am not curious about what don't concern me."

"Our warehouse?"

"That would be my guess," Jean said. "No one ever said Jacques was much of a brain. He would go where he was used to going if they asked him to store something for them."

Armand Didier's men looked at each other, plainly astounded at the news that the gold might already be in their hands, so to speak.

Friendly once more, they cut Jean free, put a cigar in his mouth and lit it for him. "Jean, you come with us and point out this Englishman who hired you. We'll buy you a new shirt on the way, quality silk."

Harvey Waller was uneasy. He paced up and down, jumped at every creak in the old warehouse timbers, cursed his brother Wilson for his slowness and stupidity. "I don't want to lose it now. You saw how easy those goddamn Pinkertons lost it. We can lose it back to them or someone else just as easy, if we aren't careful. And sitting here in this damn warehouse that this Cajun found for us—this isn't what I'd call being careful."

Doherty gave him a cold, slow, sour look. He had made the arrangements. Things seemed all right to him. "We got the Cajun here with us. Something goes wrong, he knows I'd take it out on him. I reckon we're safe enough."

Harvey grunted in scorn. "Then you aren't long for this world, young man. It's when you start getting those peaceful feelings that nothing went wrong, that's when you better keep your eyes skinned. Something always goes wrong, take my word for it. Just 'cause you and me haven't noticed it doesn't mean that it isn't there, slowly festering and getting ready to burst on us when we don't expect it. Don't let it catch you with a happy smile on your face." He strode across to peer through a crack in a boarded-up window, then returned across the vast floor of the empty warehouse. "Damn, I feel like I'm sitting here in another man's parlor. What's keeping that half-assed brother of mine? He's always been the curse on the family, from the day he was born. There's hundreds of warehouses all along the river. Why can't he rent us one and get here with a wagon in quick time? He's been gone for hours. He could be in jail or be dead by now, maybe drunk down on Canal Street—no, he'd never dare do that, I'd gut-shoot him and hang him by his heels."

Tug Yager let his boss rant on. Doherty didn't care, except when the focus of Harvey's attention turned on him. He wouldn't take criticism from any man. Jacques du Pres didn't know English well enough to follow their conversation. Doherty had gone to his home to leave pay for the men and to tell his wife not to worry, that her husband would be back in a few days. Now Jacques was beginning to wonder if he would ever see her again. He realized he should have stuck with his own kind, stayed with the devils he knew and understood. What if some of Armand Didier's men happened by and found him with these Englishmen? Armand would have no mercy. Jacques shuddered. As he well might, for the old Cajun river boss was well known to have a streak of Comanche in him when it came to tormenting an enemy.

Wilson Waller finally arrived. He had a man and

wagon outside and had found a place a little way further upriver.

This pleased Harvey. "I don't want to bring our boat anywhere near the city itself. Just like I know everything that moves on my stretch of water, so does Armand Didier. I never met the man and I don't have a thing against him—except sharing my gold with him. If we can load our boat by night upriver, we don't have to split a damn thing with him. But first we need to find ourselves a safe place to stash the gold till we can move it north. Those Pinkertons will be watching for us, too."

"This place is safe, Harvey," Wilson assured him. "I picked it close to the river and it hasn't been in use for years. I don't like the way you're talking about it in front of that Frenchie though. A lot of them understand more than they pretend to."

Harvey winked. "Doherty will look after him. After we get to the new place, you take care of that driver. Then we're clear."

"Who is it?" Doherty snarled.

"I cannot see. The faces. I cannot see." Jacques du Pres shrugged.

Doherty rapped Jacques's head against the boarded-up window as he forced him to look out the crack again.

"*Mon Dieu!* The men of Monsieur Didier, they come!"

Doherty gave him a glacial smile. "You and me have an understandin' 'bout that, don't we? You promised me this place was safe or I could take it out on you. You sly son of a bitch, you thought you could slip away in the gunfight, didn't you?"

Doherty grabbed him around the throat and started squeezing. Jacques's face turned beet red, but he was a manual worker and he ripped the gunman's hands from his neck after a brief struggle.

Surprised at being so easily overpowered, Doherty fell back on his old reliable—his Peacemaker Colt .45. He fast-drew the gun and kept it close to his own body, not giving Jacques a chance to knock it from his hand. Jacques paused and looked. He could easily have hammered home a fist into Doherty, but by the time his knuckles landed, a hot slug would be burrowing its way through him. He held back.

"On your knees," Doherty ordered. "Fast."

Jacques sank to his knees. He even tried to remember a prayer.

Doherty didn't want to fire the gun and warn Didier's men on the outside, Instead, he lashed out at Jacques's forehead with the heavy metal handgun. The first blow caught the Cajun by surprise. Doherty continued to pistol whip him until he fell to the floor. Then he used the gun butt to neatly crack his skull like an eggshell.

Through the crack in the window boards, Doherty watched the men creep forward. They would have the place surrounded and would wait to find themselves good cover before shouting out their demands. They'd offer the men inside their lives in exchange for the gold. Well, the fools had come too late. Harvey Waller had been right. Doherty was able to see that now. He had made a mistake. And that clever old fox Harvey had insisted on him waiting here till Wilson came to fetch him, leaving Doherty alone to pay for his mistake. That didn't worry Doherty, but it did give him new respect for Harvey Waller, who he had begun to think was over the hill and getting soft in the head.

He allowed Didier's men to move in closer through the overgrown wasteland around the warehouse. Then he picked up a shotgun and knocked out a board with its butt. The men outside scattered for cover.

"The gold is gone," Doherty shouted through the gap. "You're too late. Come in and take a look. The main doors ain't locked."

Silence followed his invitation. After some time, a man showed himself, clearly not too willing in this role. "What are you still here for?" he called.

"The bastards left me," Doherty shouted. "There ain't nothin' to guard. Come in and see for yourself."

Didier's man looked to one side as he took orders from another concealed man, after which he walked forward to the main doors of the warehouse, his six-gun held out warily in front of him. He didn't look as if this was his idea or as if he trusted the word of the man inside the warehouse. He swung open one of the high wooden doors to the main entrance, letting daylight flood inside. He swung open the second door and looked carefully around the interior without going in.

"The cupboard is bare," he announced. "Just this feller lying over by the window."

The other men emerged guardedly from cover, advancing with their rifles at hip level. They came in the entranceway and saw the warehouse's empty interior and the prone body close to the window with the board knocked away. They walked over to him and saw his skull cracked open, the blood beginning to crust over the wound. They realized that this couldn't have been the man who had talked to them out of the window. While they were standing there, looking at the dead man, Doherty appeared from a niche in the wall, toting his American Arms 12-gauge shotgun with cut down double barrels.

Doherty didn't pause to gloat, though he had an extra half second in which to do so. He just gave them a double load of buckshot at chest level. Then he dropped the shotgun and peered through the blue gunsmoke, Colt .45 in hand, looking for someone to move.

The large lead shot cut through all of the men standing near the window, ripping and tearing their flesh, but killed only two of them. Doherty had to reload his Colt in order to finish the wounded men off, a shot in the side of the head for each. This done, he reloaded the shotgun and went outside. The two men holding the horses were jumpy because of all the shooting they had heard inside the warehouse. He brought both of them down with a single cartridge. The horses bolted.

Doherty dragged both bodies inside the warehouse, in case someone happened by—though the warehouse was isolated on a desolate stretch of riverbank.

He looked over the pile of corpses with satisfaction. When Wilson came to fetch him—and he knew Wilson would come, because Harvey Waller needed him—he would have something to show for his time spent here. If Wilson wasn't sent to get him, Doherty himself would go after Harvey Waller, all the way upriver to St. Paul if he had to.

CHAPTER THIRTEEN

This time when Raider went to Armand Didier's house, he met a different sort of man. The flowers were still there, and the wrought-iron railings on the balconies, but Armand Didier was exuding no charm or politeness.

"You got some good men of mine killed," he barked at the Pinkerton.

"Me?"

"You! You got me into it."

Raider shook his head like he couldn't believe what he was hearing. "If I thought Armand Didier couldn't handle Harvey Waller, I wouldn't have spoken a word. It seems I made a mistake. I guess men come harder up Minnesota way than they do down here with all the soft Louisiana livin'."

"Don't you say nothing about the way folks live down here," Didier growled. "I know from the way you talk you ain't no northern carpetbagger."

"Arkansas," Raider informed him, noting that the Cajun spoke English with hardly a trace of a French accent when he felt like it.

"I wouldn't shit in Arkansas," Didier said with conviction.

"Then don't never try to cross it. It's a big state and I reckon you'd grow mighty uncomfortable."

Didier laughed and called for whiskey, not wasting his good wine on Raider. "I see you don't take offense easy. Me neither. Except when I can gain something by it. Sit down, Pinkerton, make yourself comfortable. You and me have some business to do. Some friends of mine know you by name. They tell me I should be careful how I handle you, that you're fast and mean with your gun and don't back down for no man."

"That's what I'd like to think people always say behind my back."

"I'm going to need you to handle Waller and his bunch," Didier said. "I ain't got no false pride. I just took a licking, with some of my best men dead in that warehouse. My own goddamn warehouse! It's lucky that driver who took them there, that he's dead too. I'd have won my good name back from what I'd have done to him. My reputation is damaged by this, Raider. If others see that any upriver bunch can come down here to New Orleans and kick ass, why pay me for my goodwill? My name is worth more to me than some shipment of gold, no matter how big. You get Harvey Waller for me, dead or alive, and the gold is yours. Every bar of it."

"Sounds good to me," Raider assented. "But how come you need me? You have no shortage of fast guns and muscle on the river."

"If I hire them and they fail, I've lost twice. A man in my position ain't allowed to lose that many times. Since these killings yesterday, people are starting to say how old and tired I look. I can't lose to Waller again. But if you go after him and he wipes you out, you weren't on my payroll. I don't hire no Pinkertons."

"I'll get Waller all right," Raider said. "It don't matter where he goes, he's going to keep seeing me over his shoulder. But I reckon when I do get him, I'm going to hold onto all that gold."

Didier smiled and shook his hand. "You have my word on that."

"Didier said for us to leave our money behind an' go anywhere, do anythin', we're his guests in this town," Raider told Gary Coyle and Rob Jordan back at their hotel. "He's even pickin' up our expenses here."

Rob looked shocked. "We can't allow a known criminal to subsidize our investigation in any way. Think how it would look if it became known."

To Rob's surprise, Raider immediately agreed with him. "I guess it must be one o' those Pinkerton regulations that went clean out o' my head. I believe you boys will find, like me, after years out in the field, you really need a brushup with that rulebook they have in Chicago. Pity there never seems t' be any time t' get that readin' done. I'm certain sure it would change how I go 'bout things. But you don't pay no heed to me, Rob. I reckon we won't be goin' t' the same places anyway. You'll be goin' to the cheap ones, and I'll be hittin' the fancy, expensive kind. I don't suppose our paths is goin' t' cross. What are *you* doin', Gary?"

"I was just thinkin' that if breaking one o' his regulations saved Mr. Pinkerton money for my expenses, he mightn't get so mad about it. I'll mosey along with you, Raider."

They both looked at Rob and waited.

He said, "Perhaps my interpretation of those regulations was too strict."

"That's the kind o' slippery excuse that puts you on the road t' hellfire," Raider warned him jokingly.

Rob got upset all over again because of this remark. All the same, when they went out on the town he came along with them.

New Orleans was just returning to prosperity after the collapse of trade during the Civil War. With the riots and strife of Reconstruction, it seemed New Orleans might return to being a small town on a marsh, unknown and unneeded by the outside world. Then the West began to open up. Instead of goods coming downstream, they were going up—in a richly increasing supply—to settlers, farmers, loggers, dwellers in new cities. The Mississippi had become a huge highway of men and materials, and New Orleans was at its mouth, its point of connection to the Atlantic seaboard cities and to Europe. The air of defeat, which weighed so heavily on the place when Raider last was here, had lifted now. New Orleans was back at work—and at play.

At the first place they went the maître d' did not want to let them in. When they presented themselves as guests of Armand Didier, they were shown to a corner table. Raider had some trouble with the headwaiter, who advised him not to drink bourbon with gourmet food. Raider's answer to this was to sprinkle whiskey from the bottle over his dish and then dip a crawfish in his glass of whiskey before popping it in his mouth. After that he demanded a plain fried steak and boiled potatoes, though neither was on the menu of exotic Delta dishes. After four main courses and most of the bottle of bourbon, Raider decided he was ready to move on.

Outside on the street, Gary remarked, "I'm kind of offended they didn't say they hoped to see us again soon. Ain't that what they're supposed to say?"

"I guess they must've forgot," Raider answered with a chuckle.

They hit a succession of saloons and gaming halls, ending in a bordello with plush red carpeting, flocked wallpaper, and cut crystal gaslight fixtures. Raider refused the finest of their champagnes but agreed to settle for their best brandy. He didn't have any reservations about their women: one and all were gorgeous, sexy, and willing to please these three friends of Armand Didier.

Raider climbed the staircase with a luscious black-haired Frenchwoman named Angelique. She locked the door of the room behind them and pushed him away when he tried to embrace her.

"A working girl mustn't get her clothes wrinkled," she said, turning around for him to unhook the back of her gown.

Raider's big fingers fumbled with the tiny hooks. When they were undone, she stepped out of the gown and hung it carefully in the closet. It amused him to see how much more concerned she was with where she hung her dress than where she laid her body.

She stood before him, her full breasts bulging over the top of her whalebone corset, her black-stockinged legs visible beneath lacy white petticoats. Moving her hips in a slow, seductive dance, she removed her petticoats and draped them over the back of a chair. Resting one foot on the chair, she slowly unrolled a black stocking, then did the same with the other leg. Then she opened her constricting corset and released her charms to his view.

Angelique led him to the bed. Sitting on its edge, Raider stroked her bare rump and thighs, and sucked her hardening nipples. Meanwhile she undid his shirt buttons. She lightly raked her nails across his hairy chest, then traced a line up to his jaw and ear, behind his neck and down the spine of his broad back, sending a shiver of pleasure through his body.

When Raider removed his boots, gunbelt, and pants, he saw she was impressed with his stout staff. She urged him to lie on his back on the bed, then took his stiff cock into her mouth. She sucked on him awhile, then threw a leg over and straddled him. Holding his cock in one hand, she used its swollen head to massage the moist lips of her vagina. Then she impaled herself on his erect rod and shuddered as his male meat ran into her.

Raider kissed and sucked on her breasts as they swayed before his face. He held a firm handful of each buttock and pumped her up and down on his cock. She gasped with the effort and her skin grew flushed from passion. She kept her hips bucking back and forth in an increasing frenzy, then she suddenly fell on Raider, squeezing him with her thighs while climaxing violently.

He allowed her to take her full pleasure and then rest to catch her breath before he rolled her on her back, without coming out of her, and began to deliver long slow thrusts inside her that made her mew like a kitten.

Wilson Waller carried his purchases from the store to the horse and buggy he had bought that morning. It took several trips for him to carry out the side of bacon, the sack of beans, a bag of ground coffee, tobacco, whiskey, and other staples on his list. Up until now, they had been visiting eating houses on the edge of the city, keeping away from well-known restaurants and hotels where they might be identified by Armand Didier's men. The faces of both Harvey Waller and Tug Yager were known to some of Didier's henchmen, and Harvey had no doubt their descriptions had been sent around. Neither Harvey nor

Tug looked out of the ordinary in any particular way, and there were thousands of transient strangers in New Orleans with hundreds more arriving every day, so there was no big worry they would be easily spotted. Harvey figured they would be safe enough if they kept away from the city docklands and the more central parts. That had worked well until the previous night, when only Harvey's sixth sense for trouble had saved them.

They were eating in a cheap place when two men came in and sat at a table, only to rise and leave hurriedly. In about thirty seconds Harvey had their bill paid and was hustling them out the door, still chewing on their food.

"Don't look to the left or right," Harvey ordered in the darkness outside. "Just walk along the street with me like we might be heading back to where we live."

They did as he ordered. When they had gone a short distance, Harvey took Doherty by the arm.

"My bet is one of them scumbags stayed outside the eating house to keep a watch on us. If he did, he'll be following us now. We'll make a turn at the next corner, and you hang back to see if someone comes. Don't attack some woman and kid by mistake."

"I saw them two fellers. If it's one o' them I'll know him."

"No point in wasting time or conversation with him," Harvey added.

After they turned the corner, Doherty stepped into a doorway. The other three bunched together and kept to the dark side of the street so it would be harder for someone behind them to notice they now numbered one man less. Doherty drew his boot knife, which had a honed seven-inch blade and beadwork on the handle. He never said it but he did nothing to stop people believing he had taken the weapon from an Indian brave he had killed. In reality, he had bought it from an old Mandan woman in a river town during a cold spell.

Doherty heard footsteps. A man's steps, and he was hurrying—perhaps thinking now he had lost contact with the men he was following. Perhaps someone hurrying to his wife. Doherty enjoyed killing, but he kept himself in check. He was going to make sure this was the right man, not because Harvey Waller had told him to, but for his own satisfaction. Besides, if this was not one of the two men from the eating house, it would prove Harvey wrong about being followed, and Doherty would derive a certain pleasure from that.

But it was one of the two men. He passed no more than eight feet away from Doherty, looking along the dark street for a glimpse of the men he was following.

Doherty was as light on his feet as a weasel. He was almost in arm's reach of the man when the man wheeled around, hearing something behind him. His hands were empty. Doherty hit him in the left lower chest with the blade held flat and slightly upward, so it would go in between the ribs. The steel scraped bone as it plunged in. Doherty flicked his wrist to twist the blade around inside, then pulled it out and hurried away.

He did not look to see the man stagger a few steps, support himself against a house wall, then fall forward on his hands and knees. Blood spewed from his mouth as he crawled to the front door of a house, seeking help. He never made it that far.

Wilson Waller knew none of these details—only that Doherty had taken care of their pursuer. Harvey had been careful not to go in the direction of the warehouse where they had the gold. He was still worried.

"That eating house is less than two miles from us," Harvey told him. "They'll be trawling for us hereabouts. Tug, you and me stay put inside. Doherty, you act as guard. Wilson, Armand's boys don't know you from a hole in the wall. You go fetch us what we need."

Armand Didier had given up his fancy French wine and was taking long pulls of Kentucky bourbon. He poured Raider four fingers, and the Pinkerton truthfully declared, after several serious tests, that it was the finest whiskey he had ever drunk.

"Take the bottle with you," Armand said. "I think I still have sixty cases left."

The old Cajun river boss took his time about getting around to what was on his mind. He mentioned that Raider and his comrades seemed to be having a good time on the town, judging by the bills that were starting to come in.

"I knew you'd want us to have only the best," Raider told him.

"Why not?" Didier laughed. "It's not often you Pinkertons can score off an old rascal like me. Better enjoy it while you can. But I didn't ask you here to question your taste in food, women, or drink. We caught sight of them, but they saw us and killed one of my men. It happened at the north side of the city last night."

"What makes you think they'll still be there?"

"One thing," Didier said. "I'm betting Harvey is too smart to try to move anything from the city docks. He knows I'd hear of it. Now he has to move that gold by water out of here, 'cause overland sure ain't safe or practical and we got men watching the trains like we do the boats. But there's thousands of old landing places along the river banks, and warehouses too, between here and Baton Rouge upriver.

He could use any of them and get away, if he chooses the right time. We saw him north of the city, about two miles east of the river. That's where he is; up there. He ain't coming no closer than that, and he ain't leaving neither, without dragging that gold along."

"I believe you might be right," Raider said. "How many of them?"

"Four. In an eating house. Harvey and Tug, for sure. From what you've told me, his brother Wilson was there—though none of my men know him. Plus one other."

"I'd know Wilson," Raider said.

Didier grinned and poured them each a stiff measure. "That's why I asked you here."

It was the wrong sort of tobacco, and Wilson had forgotten to buy flour. Harvey swore he had to have biscuits. While he was out, he might as well buy beer. And newspapers. In a few minutes, Wilson had another long list of purchases. He also needed to buy hay. He hadn't thought that morning they would have to keep the horse indoors. Hunger was making the animal restless. It chewed half the sleeve off Tug's coat, which had been left hanging on a nail. The only thing that saved the horse from Tug was that they couldn't risk the sound of gunfire and Tug wasn't mad enough to smear himself by cutting its throat.

Wilson harnessed the horse to the buggy. He waited for Doherty to come back from a reconnoiter outside, then drove out the main entrance. As before, he wouldn't go to any nearby stores, deliberately choosing those some distance away, just in case the storekeepers were questioned. He bought the supplies in a different store than the one he had gone to before. Now he needed hay. Wilson didn't like to ask folks questions, since that was one sure way to be noticed and remembered. When he found he was near the stables where he had bought the horse, to save himself a lot of trouble, he went back there to buy hay.

Raider was never at his best in crowded, built-up places. City people reminded him of ants, the way they ran around. Mostly they didn't take too kindly to him either, especially not to the big gun he wore openly on his hip. What looked normal on the plains, city folks found threatening. He and Gary and Rob split up to comb the area for Waller and his men. Raider sure as hell felt out of place, walking along the city streets in his western boots. He tried going in a few stores, but after the third one in a row thought he was trying to hold them up, he gave up on that. This was more in Rob and Gary's line—they were more city slickers than he was. So he walked about and tried not to frighten people by suddenly approaching them or by lingering too long in one place. When he saw the stables, with notices for horses and equipment for sale or hire, he was delighted by its familiar sight. Horses still smelled like horses, even in New Orleans.

Raider was talking to an old Arkansas boy who grew up only miles from Raider's homeplace when Wilson Waller arrived. Raider's friend excused himself.

"This feller bought that horse an' rig here this mornin'. I better go see what ails him."

Raider glanced toward the newcomer, recognized him as Wilson and eased behind a stable door before he could be noticed. He watched the stablehand fork hay into the buggy and throw a wad of it to the hungry horse. Wilson Waller handed the stablehand some coins and flicked the reins on the horse's rump. The animal reluctantly pulled the buggy out of the stable yard. Raider guessed that he could amost keep up on foot at that speed. Certainly he could give Wilson a head start and easily find him again. When Wilson was gone, Raider went to the stablehand and asked where Wilson was going.

"Dunno," the man said.

"Can you rent me a horse? He don't have to be fast, but he'll need to be able to bear my weight."

"I have an old roan stallion at a dollar a day. He's a bit contrary. You leave him untied a moment and he'll trot straight back here."

"Sounds like he's exactly what I need. Saddle him in a hurry."

Raider saw Wilson and the buggy ahead of him on the river road. That looked good. It made sense that the bastard would be headed for the river. If they intended moving the gold by water, they would keep the heavy metal near it. With a bit of luck, Wilson would lead him right to it.

The Pinkerton hung well back, which did not take much effort with his elderly horse. The city streets came to a sudden end not far ahead. The paved road with streetlights, lined with houses, turned into a muddy, rutted track between farmers' fields. Here there was no make-believe half-city half-country for wealthy residents, like there had been on the edge of St. Louis. North of New Orleans, the city just stopped as if someone had thrown down his tools and said, "Enough! Not one step farther!"

Wilson Waller took the buggy down the winding lane between the fields. Raider waited until he was out of sight before he followed. His horse was walking beside a row of willows when a man stepped from behind one of them, caught Raider by the right wrist and pulled him down out of the saddle.

Raider hit the ground on his right shoulder, awkwardly and heavily. Loose of his load, with no pressure on the bit, the horse turned around and trotted back toward home. Raider's sixgun had fallen from its holster and now lay in the mud, just out of easy reach. The man went for his gun. There was no way Raider could reach his in time, so instead, he lunged at his attacker, springing up from his prone position with an agility surprising in such a big man.

Doherty's hand was on his gun—he had been waiting here in case Wilson was trailed—and he had time to clear it from its holster. Before Doherty could point the barrel, Raider brushed the weapon aside and used the force and bulk of his body to knock his opponent down. Doherty lost his grip on his Peacemaker as he fell, but twisted out from beneath Raider and jumped to his feet again. He stooped for his weapon. Raider kicked it from his hand, and the Peacemaker slid into a wheel rut.

The two men squared off and sized each other up. The Pinkerton was much bigger and stronger. He moved confidently forward. Doherty backed away.

"I should've shot you cold in the saddle," Doherty said with regret.

"I always give a man a fightin' chance."

Doherty sneered. "No gun of Armand Didier's ever gave any man a chance."

"I ain't workin' for Didier. I'm a Pinkerton."

"Damn me, I never recognized you. Raider. I wasn't expectin' you here."

Raider could see the man was genuinely surprised. "Look, I don't want to know your name and if you deal with me, I swear I won't remember your face. What I want is the gold. You take me to it, you get to ride away. It's a fair deal. Best offer you'll get."

"I ain't ridin' nowhere, Raider. Neither of us has horses."

"You know what I mean."

"Let me think about it," Doherty said.

"Think fast. 'Cause if you don't go along, we're goin' t' settle this thing right here an' now." The Pinkerton took another step forward.

Doherty took another back. "All right. You and me, we just go there. I ain't doin' no fightin' for you."

"Nor agin me."

"I just walk away," Doherty said, and he stepped over to pick up his gun.

Raider intervened. "I reckon it's best for me t' carry that."

"If you want," Doherty agreed.

As Raider bent to retrieve the weapon, Doherty's hand slid into his boot and closed on the beaded handle of his Mandan knife. The blade snaked out and chopped at Raider's hand going for the gun. Seeing it coming too late, the Pinkerton jerked his hand away, getting only his knuckles skinned by the honed steel edge.

Doherty thrust the knife at Raider's chest in a hard straight stab. Only by jumping backward did the Pinkerton keep beyond the gleaming point. He staggered a few steps away, pulling off his leather jacket, regretting he had not brought his bowie. Wrapping the leather jacket around his left forearm elbow to hand, Raider advanced on his foe before Doherty could edge close to a gun.

Doherty prodded at him with the blade. Raider parried the thrusts with his leather-protected arm. Suddenly he came at Doherty fast, barging forward with his left forearm extended before him. Doherty stabbed viciously at him, but could not penetrate the leather with his knife nor find a way around it to the Pinkerton's body. He retreated backward before the burly Pinkerton, slashing and thrusting with the blade, hardly noticing that Raider was increasing the pace, until he stumbled backward on a root and fell.

Raider grabbed his knife hand, sank his left knee in Doherty's groin and twisted the blade toward Doherty's heart. He pressed down hard. When Doherty let go of the knife, Raider shoved it in all the way.

CHAPTER FOURTEEN

When Doherty didn't come back, Tug Yager and Wilson Waller were all for bolting as quick as they could. Harvey said no. At first he reasoned that Doherty had been offered a share of the gold and control of a whiskey-making plant upriver. But even if Armand Didier offered him more than that, Doherty wasn't fool enough to believe him. No, there was no way Doherty had gone over to the other side. Something had happened to him. The worst thing they could do now would be to allow themselves to be flushed from cover like prairie chickens only to rush into the waiting guns. The more Harvey thought about it, the more he was convinced he was right. In his opinion, Wilson had been trailed by someone and when Doherty stepped in, he had been killed or seriously hurt.

"I still say we should move out," Tug insisted. "You're right, Harvey, when you say we shouldn't let them flush us out in a hurry. But what have we got to gain by staying here, even if Doherty is dead and can't harm us? We got to move sometime."

"They know we're in this area," Wilson put in.
"They can comb the whole place looking for us. If
we give them time, they'll get to search every house
near the river. They'll find us sooner or later."

Tug hadn't shaved in a week, and his face was
covered in a thick grayish growth. Even Harvey
wouldn't have recognized him, so he said. Tug pre-
vailed on him to let him take the horse and buggy by
a different route to check what might be happening.
Since Harvey had run out of booze, he wasn't that
hard to persuade. Tug returned with no trouble to
report. Besides whiskey, he brought food and newspapers. From reports in two papers, they recognized
Doherty as the man found slain with a knife trimmed
with Indian beads. Wilson remembered the grove of
big willows and confirmed Harvey's notion that he
must have been followed.

"It won't be long now till they're banging on these
doors," Tug said ominously.

"All right," Harvey said. "Go get the boat tonight.
We'll leave tomorrow night."

After leaving Doherty's body where it fell, Raider
attempted to track Wilson's buggy on the muddy
road. The road branched many times, and there was
nothing special about the wheel tracks or hoofprints
to distinguish them from dozens of others. It wasn't
long before he gave up. Didier's men would know
this area better and might have an idea where to look.
A couple of hours passed before Raider got back into
the center of the city.

Having alerted Didier to send his men, Raider
took off for a few hours. He visited some bars and
talked with people. A few even recognized him as a
"friend" of Armand Didier's, but not as a Pinkerton
operative. He was having himself a good time when

he ran into Pinch Hogan, an outlaw who Raider knew was wanted for big-time rustling in three states and the Dakota Territory. Their eyes met and each man realized he had been recognized by the other. Raider's right hand floated over his gun handle. Pinch shook his head and slowly brought out his gun, placing it on the bar in front of Raider.

"I seen you outdraw Black Tom that time up in Cheyenne," Pinch said. "You may have slowed some since then, but I guess you're still faster than me. You gonna take me in?"

"What d' you think?" Raider asked.

"Let me finish my drink."

Raider used his own bottle to fill the man's glass. It might be a while before he had another drink.

"Didn't expect to find you in these parts," Raider said.

"You're the last son of a bitch I had hoped to see here, too."

"I didn't notice any stray beeves," Raider said. "You moved on to some other line o' work?"

"I'm hired out to Mr. Didier, who's a big businessman down here."

"Armand is a friend of mine."

Hogan's eyes rounded in surprise. "A friend?"

"That's what I said," Raider confirmed. "What d' you do for him?"

"That would be revealin' confidential . . ."

"Bullshit. Hogan, when I talk with you an' let you drink, you keep talkin' sense to me an' maybe I'll keep pourin'."

Pinch watched Raider fill his glass from the bottle again. He cleared his throat. "I do all sorts o' things. I ain't no fast gun, you know, but when it comes t' stealin' and spottin' things that can be stole, I can proudly say there's few men with the native talent I was born with. My dad was the same, so you might say it's a family thing. But I been pulled off that for the last day. I'm trampin' around lookin' for fellers by the name o' Harvey Waller, his brother Wilson, an' Tug Yager, all from a bunch upriver somewhere. I sneaked back into town. But I was plannin' to get back north o' the city in an hour or two. Then you walked in. If I hadn'ta snuck off, I'd still be a free man."

"You could still buy your way out with a trade," Raider said.

Hogan was fast. "You int'rested in the Wallers and Yager too? I reckon I could keep you posted. Can you get my warrants lifted?"

Raider shook his head. "Best I can do is fail to arrest you."

"What about report my presence here?"

"It'll be a month before I send in a report. Maybe six weeks."

"You got a deal."

Raider slid the gun and bottle along the counter to him. "If you're thinkin' 'bout runnin' or maybe doubledealin' on me, better start practicin' your draw for when we meet again."

Hogan nodded. "I remember Black Tom. . . ."

Tug Yager walked for an hour in the dark before he found someone who would hire out to drive him to Jefferson. He had left the horse and buggy in the warehouse, since they would need them to move the gold from the warehouse to the boat. It was close to midnight when he paid off the driver in Jefferson and walked down to the docks where they had moored the boat. Armand Didier controlled things here too, but not as tightly as he did in New Orleans. This far up the river, Tug reckoned they would be safe, especially since they had docked here before any troubles started or any watch was put out for them. He gave the night watchman a five-dollar gold piece, and the man rowed him out in a dinghy to Harvey's boat and helped him start the engine. He moved out to the edge of the main channel and waited for a brightly lignted riverboat heading downstream, so he could tag along. After a couple of hours wait, he followed a very large craft until he saw the lights of the city ahead.

He didn't know how, in darkness, to find the landing place he and Harvey had picked when they first arrived. They had selected the place from land, not daring to bring the boat this far south. The landing place was a solidly built wood jetty not far from the warehouse where the gold was stashed. It was used by local fisherman, who described to them the approach from the river. Tug was well aware how different a place looked from the water, and how there were usually sandbanks or shallows that had to be avoided. The approach wasn't very difficult, but because of the lack of shore lights to use as landmarks, it could not be made at night. He anchored east of the main channel and waited for first light.

When he could plainly see the church steeple and the four trees on the shore, he restarted the engines and made his approach, keeping the steeple between the third and fourth trees until he saw the big sandbank to port, then keeping the steeple between the first and second trees until he caught sight of the yellow cross painted on a rock behind the jetty. After that, he had to feel his way along a narrow channel marked by three branches stuck in the mud.

He anchored in a deep, stagnant backwater pool and paid a kid a nickel to row him ashore. He was looking forward to getting back to the warehouse in time for breakfast. Wilson would have cooked up a mess of ham and eggs and biscuits, along with terrible coffee. Then he could catch some sleep. A man his age began to feel a night spent out on the river. Not so long ago, he would have gone on all day without a wink of sleep. Now he found himself looking forward to some shuteye with the same desire he once had for other things.

Though Tug Yager was weary and his bones ached, long practice of living on the edge had taught him to keep his eyes open and his brain working. He spotted the two men following him on foot, though they kept well back. He also noticed the too-casual way a third man leaned outside a food store and didn't look in his direction. At this hour of the morning, people didn't act like it was three in the afternoon.

Tug led them away from the warehouse. He headed for an area of scraggly pines, walked in among the trees and waited there. From his coat pocket, he drew his short-barreled version of the Colt .45 Peacemaker, the one known popularly as the Sherriff's Model or Shopkeeper's Model. While Tug was no sheriff or shopkeeper, he liked the ease of handling which the short barrel gave the gun. He spun the chambers, wiped his sweaty palm on his pants and stared into the trees.

The two who had been following him guessed his game. They had no choice but to come after him—after all, there was always the chance they had not been spotted and this was where the hideout was located. They had to go in after him. But they feared the worst. They expected him to step from behind a tree at any moment with a blazing gun. So they stalked their way through the woods, twenty paces apart, revolvers cocked and held ready.

Tug steadied his gun against the tree he was hiding behind and fired at the man to the right. He nailed his victim in the gut with a single shot.

He had to step from behind the tree to find a line of sight to the second man. He heard a bullet whine past his ear as he blasted off four quick shots, scoring on the fourth. The man doubled over and fell on his side, kicking up dust as he groveled in pain. Tug looked on, well satisfied.

He caught a movement out of his left eye and whirled around. Tug saw the third man, who had been lounging outside the food store. He had come at Tug from the side. Tug snapped back the hammer, fired fast and missed. His adversary fired at him and missed also, the bullet whacking into a pine next to him. Tug pulled the trigger again, but this time the hammer fell on a spent shell. He had fired his six shots.

The gunman emptied his weapon at Tug. He connected with the fourth and sixth shots, hitting the stocky riverman with both bullets in the upper chest.

With shaking hands, Pinch Hogan stuffed live cartridges into the chambers of his smoking gun. Then he cautiously checked to make sure Tug Yager was dead. So too were the two men who had come with him.

Pinch was shaking so badly he barely managed to unbutton his pants in time to empty his bladder. This was not at all his style of work. He swore out loud while he was pissing that he was going to take a coach to Texas come next pay.

Raider had finished a steak, four eggs, and two quarts of beer for breakfast and his mood was improving somewhat when he spotted Pinch Hogan in the hotel lobby. Pinch knew his room number. It mightn't be too healthy for Pinch if he and the Pinkerton were seen together. In Raider's room, where Rob and Gary joined them, Hogan bought his freedom with valuable information.

"I just come from Mr. Didier's," Hogan told them, recounting how the night watchman at the Jef-

ferson dock had sent a telegram to New Orleans and
Didier had placed men at every landing stage in the
city and for some miles north of it. He explained
what happened. "Mr. Didier cussed me out for not
takin' Tug alive. He says it's a waste of time lookin'
in them pine woods. He's changed his plans. What
he wants us t' do now is let the two Waller boys put
the gold on that boat—even help 'em any way we
can by stoppin' people interferin' with 'em or whatever. Just so long as the Wallers don't know we're
doin' it. Once that gold is on the water, Mr. Didier
says it's all his. Hell, I didn't even know till a half
hour ago there was any gold involved. Mr. Didier
will have boats standin' by to take care o' things
when them two Wallers put out on the river."

Raider nodded. "I'm no match for Armand on the
water."

Raider assumed he was being watched. He waited at
the fishing dock, holding a package, and trying to
figure which boat was Harvey Waller's. He could tell
two horses apart that might seem identical to a city
man, but all boats of similar length looked the same
to him. A kid in a dinghy ferrying some people told
him to wait, he would be back. When he came,
Raider stepped into the dinghy. He would have
tipped it over except for the kid's fast movements to
balance it. The kid waited for the little boat to stop
rocking before he spoke.

"Where to, mister?"

"Mr. Waller's boat."

"Who?"

"Harvey Waller."

"He don't have no boat here, mister."

Raider held up a silver dollar. "Strangers from up
north. It ain't been here long."

"No way, mister. Not if you paid me fifty dollars."

"So row me out anyways," Raider said.

"Where to?"

"Just out on the river."

"What for?"

Raider looked at him like he couldn't believe he was so dumb. "Hell, surely you don't expect me to shoot you this close to shore?"

The kid got a funny look on his face and straightaway began working the oars. He headed for a good-sized grey motorboat without masts. Raider took out a gold watch he had borrowed from Rob.

"You want me to come back for you, mister?" the kid asked when the dinghy came alongside the motorboat.

"No, kid. You ain't goin' to strand me out here. Tie up to it and climb aboard ahead o' me."

The kid didn't argue. Raider climbed onto the deck after him and consulted his watch again. Then he did some mental arithmetic and measured out double armspans of fuse. He went down to the bottom of the cockpit and lifted some boards next to the engine. Having opened the package, he inserted a firing cap into one of the three dynamite sticks bound together. He attached the fuse to the cap and stuffed the dynamite between the floor and one part of the engine that stuck out. Having stretched out the fuse to its full length, he struck a match and lit its end. The fuse sizzled and turned to ash inch by inch. When Raider looked up, the kid was gone.

Up on the deck, the Pinkerton watched the kid head for shore, already about thirty yards away. The kid was facing him, furiously working the oars, a grin on his face. Raider drew his Remington .44 and snapped back the hammer.

"You going to shoot a kid, mister?"

"I don't have to," Raider called. "I can put a few slugs in your waterline and you'll be swimmin' like a muskrat. You want to lose your boat?"

"You must be some shot," the kid hollered cheerfully, now forty yards away.

"Look at your left oar." Raider raised the pistol to eye level, fired, and cut a groove close to the kid's hand.

"Hold on, mister," the kid yelled. "I'm comin' back for you. That silver dollar still good?"

"Sure."

Raider went below again and pinched off the fuse. He took some more out, twisted on the addition and relit the end. He watched it a few seconds to make sure it was burning true. When he went up on deck this time, the kid was waiting for him.

Halfway over to the jetty, Raider produced two silver dollars and asked, "You know a place to land a bit downriver so we don't have to go in to the jetty?"

"Sure, mister."

"Hold on till the last minute, so it looks like we mean to land at the jetty."

The dinghy was touching shore when Waller's boat blew up, stuck its snout in the air like a drowning steer and slowly disappeared.

CHAPTER FIFTEEN

Wilson broke down when Tug did not return. "We're disappearing one by one," he wailed.

"Pity it wasn't you instead of him," Harvey snarled. "I still got you as a millstone around my neck."

"You rotten son of a bitch, you always wanted to see me dead, just because Momma was always partial to me."

"We've all been picking up after you, Wilson, all your life. I get tired of it at times. Don't push me now. Tug was my right-hand man. I don't have another man near the same caliber as him. I'll sorely miss him if he's gone."

"You think he's joined Didier too?"

Harvey clenched his fists and took a few steps toward Wilson in blind rage before he gained control of himself. "Neither Tug nor Doherty were turncoats. They were loyal to me. Maybe that cost them their lives. Doherty certainly. Tug would die for me. The only turncoat ever steps near me is my own brother. Explain that to me!"

Wilson had other concerns. "I guess you'll be

saying to me shortly, 'Go out and buy me a newspaper.' That way you'll be rid of me. Then you can die here alone with all the gold. You won't mind that, Harvey. You'll die happy 'cause you still held onto all the gold." Harvey started laughing, and this unexpected turn only upset Wilson more. "What are you laughing about? Something terrible is going to happen to me. That's the only thing that'd make you laugh like that."

"I'll tell you what I'm laughing about," Harvey said calmly. "You and me are sitting here on more gold than some people know exists in the world. We're surrounded by the gunsels of a river boss who'd make a snake look good. Everyone who came with us is dead. And what do we do? We quarrel with one another like we did when we were kids at home. If that doesn't make you laugh, you've got no sense of humor."

"That doesn't make me laugh, and nothing you've ever done in your life has anything to do with a sense of humor. I don't want to die. I want to get out of here alive. With that gold!"

"Spoken like a true Waller. Wilson, I'm beginning to like the way you sound. You and me are going to move that crap out of here and live in luxury the rest of our lives."

Wilson nodded. "That's what I want."

"That's what you're going to have, boy. Stick with me. I been thinking. My guess is they've set up something with our boat. Killed Tug but left it at the landing place hoping we'll use it anyway, 'cause we got nothing else. Well, they got too low of an opinion about my intelligence. These Southerners, especially the French-speaking ones, think themselves a cut above normal. They like to think they're always three steps ahead of you and that you'll plod on and do what they expect. That pride has undone them often enough, but they don't learn from it."

"What'll we do?" Wilson asked, knowing his brother could carry on for an hour without going into any details.

"Tomorrow morning, I'll leave with the horse and buggy, trade them in, and hire a driver with a strong team and wagon, along with two good riding horses for me and you. We'll load the gold, cover it with a canvas sheet and let the driver take it by road up to Baton Rouge. Me and you will go different ways, traveling separately, and be waiting there for him. Then, just like regular folks, we'll board a riverboat in Baton Rouge bound for St. Louis, taking our cargo on board with us. Armand Didier doesn't control things up there."

Next morning, as soon as Harvey was gone, Wilson left too. He got a ride into the city on a freight wagon carrying firewood. He read the driver's newspaper to pass the time and saw a front-page item about three men shot to death in a pine wood. From the descriptions, one sounded like Tug. On another page, there was an account of the explosion and sinking of a steamboat. Wilson thought he recognized that one also. Armand Didier's men were tightening their stranglehold hour by hour. In the city, he headed straight for a shipping office.

"When can I sail for New York?" Wilson asked.

"Four, tomorrow afternoon, sir."

"Give me a ticket. One way."

To avoid the possibility of meeting his brother on the road and being asked where he had been, Wilson took a shortcut through an old graveyard next to the warehouse. If Harvey was already back, he could claim he had just been passing time by reading the names on the headstones. But he was back at the warehouse an hour before his brother returned.

"How did it go?" Wilson asked.

"The wagon arrives at daybreak tomorrow, along with two horses. The driver will bring two men to help us load."

"It's risky, Harvey. I don't like the sound of it. Word of it will get to Didier."

"Naw, not from this driver. He never heard of Armand Didier. He's a good old country boy."

"You told him where to come?" Wilson asked.

"Hell, no. I meet him down by the river, where this road meets the one going north, where that big old schooner is busted up in the reeds. I told him it was valuable furniture I wanted moved to a big house on the east side of Lake Pontchartrain. It'll be soon enough to tell him where he's going after the two helpers are gone."

Harvey had seen the newspapers too and had come to the same conclusion as Wilson, though the latter had to pretend to be hearing the news for the first time.

"What happens when we get back to St. Paul?" Wilson asked.

"What do you mean, what happens?"

"With the gold," Wilson said. "There's only two of us left now. You agree to split it fifty-fifty?"

Harvey just laughed at him and didn't say a word.

"You know I'm getting tired of being treated as a good-for-nothing idiot brother," Wilson told him. "It's high time I took a fair cut. Half that gold is mine."

Harvey looked at him like he was a mangy dog. "You're lucky I feed you and give you a roof to sleep under. You don't earn a cut of anything. You tried to steal that gold while it was on my part of the river. If another man who wasn't my brother had done that, I'd have him shot. Me just putting up with you and not squashing you like a bug, which you deserve to be, that's reward enough. You're dang fortunate I swore to our mother on her deathbed I'd look after you when you came out of jail. That's the only reason I'm doing it. I want you to know that."

"Well, you don't have to do it any longer, Harvey."

Harvey's face brightened. "You going to stay on down here?"

"Not me," Wilson said. "But you are."

Harvey stared at the gun in his brother's hand. He listened to its hammer being cocked. "Don't be a fool, Wilson. You can't make it on your own. You think I'm hard on you and don't give you your due. Then wait till you're on your own. See what happens when I'm not around to look out for you. You ended up in the clink after what you did in the bank. You'll end dancing in the air with a rope necktie if you squeeze that trigger."

"I got it all worked out, Harvey," Wilson grinned. He was enjoying this. It was much easier to do than he thought. "I'm going to New York, put that gold in a Broadway bank and live like a gentleman in a townhouse. In a year, I'll have forgot you ever existed."

Harvey took a step nearer and Wilson fired the gun. The bullet struck Harvey in the gut. The force of the projectile lifted him off his feet and dumped him on his back on the floor. He moaned with pain and looked up at his brother, who was still pointing the smoking gun at him.

"Get me help fast, Wilson," Harvey croaked.

"Why? So you can get better and take your revenge on me? I'm not as much a fool as you take me for."

Wilson squeezed the trigger again. This time the

bullet entered Harvey's right eye and killed him instantly.

Wilson stared down at him a while. Finally, he spoke out loud to his dead brother. "Funny, I thought I was going to be a bit upset about this part."

Pinch Hogan found Raider in a riverside tavern. "I saw one of your young Pinkerton pards back along the road. He told me sooner or later I'd find you here."

"I ain't much for walkin' around botherin' people with questions," Raider said sourly. "What do you have for me?"

"Maybe somethin', maybe nothin'. It's hard to tell."

"What is it?" Raider asked, already liking the sound of it.

"First, I'd like t' know where I stand with you," Pinch said. "I gave you good information on that boat. I heard it was you who blew it up, right under the noses of Mr. Didier's men. Mr. Didier was mad as hell. I don't think he wants to talk with you no more."

"He smells gold too strong," Raider said. "All right, you bought your way out of me arrestin' you with that. What d' you want for this? You want t' put somethin' on account?"

"In case I run into you in the future?" Pinch inquired.

Raider nodded and poured him a drink.

"That would be a sensible plan," Hogan said seriously, as if he were talking about putting money in the bank. "A little somethin' for a rainy day. Here's what I got. Mr. Didier says the Wallers will have to hire a wagon to move that gold. All the drivers have t' pay him t' be allowed t' work the docks, so we know most of 'em an' they've been on the lookout, with a big cash reward promised t' the man who turns 'em in. But up here, at the edge o' the city, I found some drivers who do nearly all country runs and hardly come into New Orleans at all. Now, Harvey Waller bein' a river boss himself and knowin' how things go, it makes sense that this would be the kind o' man he would use t' move the gold. One o' these drivers has been asked t' bring two men t' load heavy furniture for tomorrow, first thing. When the driver asked where t' come, the man who hired him—a stocky man with a red face, which sounds like Harvey himself, don't it—anyway, this man insists on meetin' the driver by the side o' the road. That ain't reg'lar, the driver tells me, and he wants t' charge extra if this feller is a smuggler or somebody illegal. I told him he had every cause to."

"It has the right feel about it," Raider granted Hogan.

Pinch said proudly, "I have a nose for that kind o' thing."

"And you won't pass this along t' Didier?"

Hogan paused. "That will mean another deposit in my account."

Raider grunted assent and passed the bottle.

Wilson met the driver with his two helpers and the wagon and two saddled horses at first light near where the old schooner was rotting on the riverbank. The driver argued about rates and demanded money in advance. Wilson gave it to him. Then he led them to the warehouse, opened its big doors, and pointed to the three crates that needed moving. The four men loaded them onto the wagon.

"All right, I'm going to pay you two now, so you can go," Wilson said to the two helpers.

"I guess we'll ride along part of the way," one said.

"No, you won't," Wilson said. "Here's your money. Now, both of you go."

To Wilson's horror, one pulled a gun. This man said, "I'm Pinkerton operative Rob Jordan. This is my partner Gary Coyle. You're under arrest for robbery, Mr. Waller, and I understand that other charges may later be lodged against you."

"You're with Raider?" Wilson asked in a tiny, astonished voice.

"He's waiting just down the road for us," Rob said. "He didn't figure his using a disguise would fool you, so he stayed out of sight. Where's your brother, Mr. Waller?"

"I'll tell Raider, not you."

"If you like," Rob said agreeably. "Hand over your gun."

Wilson did not do so, but made no effort to interfere with Rob taking it from him. He walked meekly alongside the wagon as the horses pulled it out of the warehouse. Down the road a piece, without being noticed, he managed to untie one of the saddle horses from the side of the wagon. He stepped into one stirrup and whacked the horse. Clinging to the saddle and the horse's mane, he got a start on the two Pinkertons. They both drew their revolvers and leveled them.

"Don't shoot," Rob commanded. "We got the gold. He won't get far."

"Let me chase him down on that other horse," Gary said.

"I need you with me to protect the gold. This place is crawling with Didier's men. It's not Wilson we need to worry about. Where the hell is Harvey? Hiding behind that big tree yonder, with a Remington repeater in his hands?"

"I don't know what the hell is going on here and I don't like it much," the driver muttered to his horses.

Raider met them on the road. He said, "A rider passed me at a gallop. He had his head down but I'm nearly sure it was Wilson. You let him get away?" When Gary and Rob nodded, he said, "Damn, I wanted to take him upriver to hang for a killin' there. No sign o' Harvey?" They shook their heads. "Let's take that gold into the bank first and then start thinkin' 'bout them. You looked in the crates?" Again they shook their heads. "Lets do it now."

The first two crates were full of rocks. In the third, they found the one-eyed corpse of Harvey Waller grinning up at them.

Raider sat in total darkness on a stone near the warehouse, intending to remain motionless there all night. He, Rob, and Gary had spent the daylight hours searching for the gold bars, without finding a trace of them. They had to be close by. If they were, it stood to reason Wilson would come for them. While Rob and Gary slept in the hotel back in the city, Raider set himself a lonely vigil.

He tried to work out what had happened and decided that Wilson, after killing his brother, had correctly suspected that their arrangements with the driver would become known. He must have panicked and hit on some other method of disposing of the gold. But since he used the driver to remove Harvey's body from the warehouse, that meant he didn't want people finding a body there and snooping around—which could mean the gold was hidden somewhere close by, to be collected at some later, safer time.

Yet Wilson had not much time in which to hide the gold. What had he done with it? They couldn't find it. Tomorrow they would try again, extending their search over a wider area. Meanwhile, at least, Raider felt he was physically close to what he was looking for. He sat very still in the blackness, with the stars overhead, hearing animals rustle in the undergrowth and distant dogs bark.

He had been there for four hours, stiff and cold, when he thought he heard the scrape of metal. He tensed and listened intently. Then he heard it again. The sound wasn't coming from the warehouse, but from a place down the road a bit.

Raider moved silently along the dirt road, all the while hearing the scraping sound get louder and closer. He saw the form of something close by and his hand dropped to his gun. But it was only a large headstone in an old graveyard. He listened again and heard the scraping sound. Now he knew what it was. Someone was digging a grave in there in total darkness. Raider moved silently among the headstones toward the sound.

Accustomed to the dark, his eyes made out the figure of a man digging with a spade. Raider moved close to him and put his hand on the man's right arm.

The man's body stiffened and he stared at the hand on his arm without turning around. "Harvey!" he croaked and fell forward into the hole he had been digging.

Raider's feet bumped against things. He picked one up. A gold bar. They were lying all around him in the long grass.

"Come on, Wilson, let's go," Raider said, helping him out of the hole.

Wilson did not cooperate. Raider set him on the grass and struck a match. Wilson's face was contorted in a look of terror. He was no longer breathing. There was fear in his sightless eyes.

SONS OF TEXAS

Book one in the exciting new saga of America's Lone Star state!

TOM EARLY

Texas, 1816. A golden land of opportunity for anyone who dared to stake a claim in its destiny...and its dangers...

Filled with action, adventure, drama and romance, *Sons of Texas* is the magnificent epic story of America in the making...the people, places, and passions that made our country great.

Look for each new book in the series!

188